Ballet Stars

Dear Reader,

Ballet has always been a very important part of my life, something I've shared with friends and practised just for myself. It's the first thing I want to do when I feel great, and something that always makes me feel better if I'm having a bad day. Learning new steps is fun, and practising a dance until you get it right can give you a big sense of achievement. And performing for an audience is the greatest feeling in the world!

I hope you'll enjoy reading about the dancing adventures that Tash and her friends have in **Ballet Stars**, and that the stories might inspire you to get up and dance yourself. I know, if you do, you'll have loads of fun.

Lots of love,

Jane Lawes

www.janelawes.co.uk

For the ballet teachers who have taught me to dance – and,
more importantly, taught me to love to dance

First published in 2015 by Usborne Publishing Ltd.,
Usborne House, 83-85 Saffron Hill, London EC1N 8RT, England.
www.usborne.com

Copyright © Jane Lawes, 2015

The right of Jane Lawes to be identified as the author
of this work has been asserted by her in accordance with the
Copyright, Designs and Patents Act, 1988.

Cover: illustration of dancers by Barbara Bongini;
pattern of flowers © Nataliia Kucherenko/Shutterstock

The name Usborne and the devices ♀ ⊕ are Trade Marks of
Usborne Publishing Ltd.

A CIP catalogue record for this book is available from the British Library.

JFMAMJJ SOND/17   03459/2   ISBN 9781409583530
Printed in India.

Usborne
Ballet
Stars

Perfect
Pirouette

Jane Lawes

USBORNE

Chapter 1

The evening sunlight flashed between the trees, forcing Tash to put a hand up to shield her eyes. The motorway looked just like any other. She was impatient for the moment when they'd turn off onto smaller roads, past fields, houses with quaint names like Rose Cottage, and pretty churches. Somewhere at the end of one of those little roads was another turning. It led to big iron gates and a long gravel drive, and at the end of the drive was an old mansion set in beautiful gardens. This was Tash's first day at Aurora House, one of the best ballet schools in the country, and she was going to be late.

"Can't we go a bit faster?" she asked.

"Only if you want me to get fined for speeding," Mum replied, grimacing at Tash. "Sorry, darling. I'll get you there as soon as I can."

"I know," sighed Tash. "It's not your fault."

Mum had got held up with something important at work. On a *Sunday*. But Tash couldn't complain. Mum ran her own business and she worked really hard to keep it going. Tash had got a scholarship to Aurora House so they didn't have to pay the school fees, but there was still the school uniform and PE kit to buy, not to mention ballet shoes and leotards!

Tash had never been as excited about anything in her entire life as she was about Aurora House. She'd dreamed of becoming a dancer since she was six years old and now she was about to begin

her first year at a full-time ballet school. ᴅ⸺
every day was going to be complete and total
heaven!

She'd liked her junior school and she'd had
friends there, but doing ballet outside school twice
a week just wasn't enough for Tash. She wanted to
dance all the time. She'd still have to do school
lessons like maths and English at Aurora House,
but she could definitely put up with that because
there'd be ballet classes every day. And – even
better – everyone else at the school would be
ballet-mad too.

Maddy, her best friend from junior school, was
funny and kind, and they liked going shopping
together and playing games in the playground,
but she didn't really *get* ballet. She could never
understand why Tash wanted to spend hours
repeating the same exercises over and over again,
moving her legs and arms and feet in patterns and
positions with weird French names. Tash had tried
so many times to explain how ballet made her feel

– that it was like everything else in the whole world just stopped and it was only her body and the music, and when she got something just right it felt like the purest kind of perfection. But Maddy always looked at her as if she was crazy. Tash would miss Maddy *loads* while she was away at school, but she knew that the girls in her class at Aurora House would understand all the things her friends at home hadn't.

Tash had auditioned for a few full-time ballet schools, but Aurora House was the one she'd desperately wanted. Her favourite ballet company was City Ballet – she had a book all about the company's biggest stars, and she'd spent hours watching video clips of them dancing. One of the company's original stars was Abigail Hartley – she'd danced the leading role in every ballet they performed, and she'd been especially famous for *The Sleeping Beauty*. When she retired in 1965 she'd started Aurora House Ballet School so that she could pass on everything she knew to the next generation of dancers. And all Tash wanted was to learn to dance like her.

Abigail Hartley was eighty-five now, so the school was run by the headteacher, another retired City Ballet dancer, James Watkins. Mr Watkins had been at Tash's audition. She remembered the day so clearly – how his stern face had made her feel a bit afraid of him as she stood in front of the panel of teachers in her plum-coloured leotard, her candidate number (104) pinned on the front and back. But despite her nerves, she'd felt thrilled, too. She almost hadn't been able to believe it was really happening; she'd watched the famous James Watkins dancing so many times in YouTube videos and on some of her DVDs, and now he was sitting there watching *her* dance!

The audition had taken place in a big studio at the school, which had felt very far away from the church hall and the portable *barre* Tash was used to for ballet classes. This studio felt serious and professional; dancers who came here meant to do ballet for a career. Looking around her, Tash had seen that there were a lot of girls her age who wanted that – everyone looked determined to get a place at the school. And only twelve of them would. The tension filled the studio as they all stood still, trying not to let their fear escape in nervous little movements. Finally one of the teachers began to lead them through the steps they needed to demonstrate. They danced through most of the exercises together, only splitting into smaller groups when they came to the sequences in the centre.

The first sequence was a slow, graceful exercise of *chassés*, *arabesques* and lovely arm movements, and as Tash was in the second group she got a chance to watch some of her competition before it was her turn. She saw straight away that most of the dancers were as good as she was. Tash needed a full scholarship to the school; to get it, she would have to dance better than she'd ever danced before.

When her turn came, she stepped into her place in the centre of the middle row and began to dance. The combination wasn't difficult, but making it absolutely perfect while also smiling and trying to make it look easy was *hard*. Luckily, smiling while dancing came naturally to Tash, and halfway through the sequence she realized that she was actually enjoying herself.

After that, the rest of the audition went very fast. Tash did a simple *pirouettes* exercise, some small, bouncy jumps on the spot and an exhilarating routine of bigger leaps travelling across the room. Then she had to have a physical check with the school doctor, who prodded her feet and measured how tall she was, and finally she had an interview with the panel of judges. This was even scarier than the dance part of the audition and she remembered it vividly.

"Why do you want to be a dancer?" Mr Watkins had asked.

"When I dance..." Tash began hesitantly,

"there's nothing except the music and the feeling of my body stretching and working. When I get the steps exactly right, I feel like I could do anything in the world! And when I watch a really great dancer, like Tamara Rojo at English National Ballet, or the dancers at the Royal Ballet and City Ballet, and they do something perfectly, it's like nothing else in the world matters at all... because in that moment, *everything's* perfect. That feels amazing. And...I want to make people feel like that."

She laughed, embarrassed, but Mr Watkins smiled.

"I understand," he said.

Suddenly, Tash's imagination leaped to a picture of Mr Watkins as a young dancer in the City Ballet, and she felt a little less afraid of him. A long time ago he must have been just like her – trembling with nerves at an audition for a ballet school!

* * *

"Off the motorway at last!" said Mum, pulling Tash back to the present.

Tash turned away from the window and smiled at her.

"You're very quiet," Mum went on. "Feeling nervous?"

"Just thinking," said Tash. "I hope the other girls will be friendly."

Although she'd met some other dancers her age at the audition, she wouldn't know who else had got a place until she arrived at the school.

"I'm sure they will," said Mum. "You're all in the same boat, everyone's moving away from home for the first time."

Tash nodded and looked out of the window again. She felt a bit guilty for going away to school and leaving Mum all by herself. Tash's dad had left when she was just a baby, and she didn't have any brothers or sisters. She'd never minded that much; it had always been just Tash and Mum, and that was how she liked it. But Mum was going to be lonely without her, she knew. And she'd be lonely without Mum. How would she get through the next seven weeks without their special chats at breakfast time and while they made dinner together, or their cosy film nights, or singing along to the radio together on the way to and from Tash's ballet classes? Suddenly half-term seemed a long way off.

She sat up straighter in her seat and forced herself to think positive thoughts. Moving away from home when you were only eleven years old was tough, but it was what you had to do if you wanted to be a great ballerina. And Tash wanted that more than anything in the world – way more than she wanted to turn around and go back to her cosy house and familiar church-hall ballet class.

They were turning in to the school grounds now. The building was old and impressive, and it looked more like the kind of place lords and ladies would live than a school. Trees lined the long drive along both sides, their leaves rustling in the cool September air. Tash peered at it all as Mum pulled the car into a space near the entrance. The second she stepped out of the car, her life would change for ever.

"Come on," she said, trying to sound more confident than she felt. It was seven o'clock and they'd been told to arrive at half past five. They were seriously late.

"Here we go," said Mum.

Tash got out of the car and helped Mum get the suitcases from the boot. The gravel sounded loud under their feet. When they reached the school's main entrance, Tash pushed open the heavy wooden door and stepped hesitantly inside.

The entrance hall seemed larger and grander than Tash remembered. The floor was tiled, dark blue and cream, and paintings and old City Ballet posters in frames decorated the walls. There was even an old fireplace, which was filled with flowers. Photographs of Aurora House students onstage and in costumes covered the wall around it.

A woman came bustling out of the office near the front door.

"You're very late!" she said briskly. "What's your name?"

"Natasha Marks."

The receptionist made a quick note on her register. Tash looked worriedly up at Mum, who pulled a face while the receptionist wasn't looking. Tash felt the urge to laugh, but she tried to hide it.

"Come on, I'll sneak you in at the back of the dining hall," the receptionist said, her face softening into a smile. "Don't worry. You haven't missed Ms Hartley's talk yet." She waved a hand at Tash's suitcases. "You can leave your things here and take them upstairs later. The others have already been to their dormitories."

The receptionist hurried them along the corridor. They could hear the babble of voices in the distance, and the closer they got to the dining room, the louder the noise became. Tash glanced anxiously at Mum. It was scary enough coming to a new school, scarier still when you were going to be living there. Now she had to walk into a room full of the whole school and their parents, late, showing everyone that she was already messing up on her first day. Right at that moment, she wished she could turn around and go home.

But the receptionist gave her no choice. She opened the door and ushered Tash and Mum inside.

The room was big with high ceilings and long wooden tables. Most of the tables were full of girls and boys chatting, laughing and shrieking as if they'd never get to talk again. An elderly woman at the teachers' table, who Tash recognized as Abigail Hartley, stood up and clinked her glass with her knife. The room fell silent immediately, with Tash and Mum still standing in the doorway.

"Oh!" said Ms Hartley, seeing Tash. "Are you late, dear? Please hurry up and sit down."

Tash went red and moved towards the nearest empty chair as the entire school turned to stare at her. She scrunched her body down as small as possible on the seat, wishing she could slide under the table and get away from everyone's eyes. She'd only been at Aurora House for five minutes – what if she'd already made a bad impression on the school's founder?

Chapter 2

Mum sat down opposite Tash at the table nearest the door, which was full of girls and boys about Tash's age, all looking around them with awe in their eyes – obviously the new Year Sevens – and their parents. Some of them were still watching Tash, but then Ms Hartley began to speak and all eyes fixed on the elegant old woman.

"Here we are, another new term at Aurora House! I'm welcoming some of you to the school for the very first time" – she smiled in the direction of Tash's table – "but for most of you this is a welcome back after the long summer holidays. A lot of you have heard all this before. But you know that you're going to hear it again because I tell the same story at the beginning of every year.

"When I was only nineteen I danced the role of Aurora in *The Sleeping Beauty* with City Ballet. As I ran out onto the stage, I thought it was the proudest moment of my life. I thought that whatever came afterwards, nothing could ever top that feeling. Remembering that, when I retired from ballet and founded this school, I named it Aurora House after my greatest moment onstage."

Tash smiled, thinking about Ms Hartley as a young ballerina. It was easy to imagine – even though she was old now, she still stood like a dancer, with her head held gracefully up and her arms elegantly at her sides. She was a tiny woman, but she could command the whole room into silence, and Tash already wanted to impress her.

"But I was wrong about that moment," Ms Hartley continued. "The proudest day of my life happens every year, when I see another class of students leave this school and begin their lives as professional dancers around the world. We said goodbye to a class of talented eighteen year olds at the end of last summer term. But I see that, once again, we've found some equally talented eleven year olds to take their places."

She paused and smiled over at Tash's table again.

"It's extremely difficult to get into this school, so congratulations to you all. But I'm afraid the hard work is only just starting. You'll all follow your own paths, of course, but I know that at the end of them, you'll make me very proud. I hope you make yourselves proud too."

Ms Hartley sat back down to a riot of clapping and cheering from the school. As everyone settled into chatting again, a teacher directed Tash and Mum to the serving point at the other end of the room to get some food, which everyone else was already busily eating. When she sat back down with a plate of chicken, rice and vegetables, Tash realized that most of the parents were having lively conversations about classes and companies and training.

Tash looked down at her food and concentrated very hard on cutting up the chicken. She and Mum were out of place here. Mum always loved watching Tash dance, but she didn't know the names of steps like these parents did and she didn't know much about the history of City Ballet, the company that the school was associated with. Tash tuned in to a conversation between two girls further down the table. They were talking about the City Ballet's junior summer classes, which they'd obviously done together. She wondered what their ballet training had been like so far. She bet it didn't include a draughty church hall and a wobbly portable *barre*. Mum was wrong – everyone wasn't in the same boat at all. Tash wasn't sure that *her* boat was even on the same ocean.

She thought back to the day she'd come home from school to find a letter waiting for her on the kitchen table with the Aurora House logo on the envelope. She'd felt so nervous that she almost couldn't open it. She waited until after she'd had dinner, and then she waited until she'd helped Mum with the washing-up, and then she waited for no reason other than putting it off in case it was a no. Eventually she peeled back the sticky seal of the envelope and pulled out a sheet of paper. She only got as far as *Dear Natasha, We are pleased to offer you a full scholarship*...before she'd screamed and thrown the sheet of paper in the air, grabbing Mum by the hands and pulling her away from her laptop.

"I'm going to ballet school! I'm going to *Aurora House!*"

Mum hugged her and they danced around together, and when Tash finally tore herself out of Mum's arms and dived down to the floor to rescue the letter and envelope she saw that Mum was crying.

"What's the matter?" she asked.

"I'm so proud of you." Mum laughed and brushed the tears away from her eyes. "You're so wonderful. And you're *my* little girl."

Tash had nearly cried then, too. It was a lot to take in. She'd got a place at Aurora House – she was going to go away to a full-time ballet school and dance every day, and if she worked really, really hard, one day she'd be a ballerina.

"We need to celebrate," said Mum. "News like this calls for the best."

Tash grinned and settled into her favourite armchair to read the rest of the letter while Mum made them both mugs of the fancy, only-for-special-occasions hot chocolate she'd brought back from a trip to Paris.

A smile spread over Tash's face while she remembered all this. Mum might not know everything about ballet like the other parents did, but she *did* care just as much about Tash's dancing dreams.

One of the teachers who'd been at the audition had come over to their end of the table and was talking to the two parents nearest Tash.

"Hello, Danielle," the teacher said to the girl sitting with them. Danielle looked very small for an eleven year old, and had light blonde hair pulled up into a ponytail. Her blue eyes were the same colour as the forget-me-not flowers that sprang up in Tash and Mum's garden every spring. Tash blinked hurriedly – she did not want to think about her garden or about home.

"It's great to see you here as an Aurora House student at last," continued the teacher.

"Thanks," the girl replied. "But *please*, please call me Dani! No one ever says Danielle. Do you know who the sixth girl in our dorm is? There was a spare bed when we went up earlier."

"I have no idea about dormitories," laughed

the teacher. "I'm just here to make sure your pirouettes are perfect." She turned to Tash. "Hi. Natasha, right? I remember you from the audition. I'm Miss Anderbel. I'm very pleased to see you here."

She gave Tash a lovely smile and for a moment Tash forgot that she felt like an outsider.

"Thanks," Tash said, remembering that Miss Anderbel had been a principal dancer at City Ballet for a few years, before an injury had forced her to give up dancing on stage. It was amazing that so many of her new teachers had once been stars of the ballet world! "I'm really happy to be here, too," she added.

"Well, I'll leave you girls to chat," said Miss Anderbel. "I'll see you in the studio tomorrow."

Tash grinned at Dani almost automatically at the mention of the studio, but as soon as Miss Anderbel was gone Dani started a conversation with a boy and a girl sitting on her other side.

"I hope we get to dance in the Hartley

studio tomorrow," she said. "That's the biggest one."

Tash wondered how Dani could possibly know so much already. Had being late really put her so far behind all of the others?

After they'd finished eating, Tash and Mum went back to the entrance hall to take Tash's suitcases up to her dormitory. The receptionist led the way, talking all the time about the history of the school and the famous dancers who had trained there. As Tash listened, she gazed at the paintings and photographs that lined the walls of the grand old staircase.

Tash's dormitory was a pretty, light room with big windows at one end and three beds down each side. Five of them were already made up with brightly coloured duvet covers and piled with bags and clothes. It suddenly hit Tash that she'd have to sleep in this strange room tonight instead of her familiar bed at home and she started to worry about how much she'd miss Mum. She put her suitcases down by the last bed and Mum helped her to put the lilac-and-white flowery cover and pillowcases she'd brought from home on the duvet and pillows. Once they'd done that, the bed looked much more like it was hers and she felt better about the idea of sleeping in it.

The other Year Sevens were saying goodbye to their parents downstairs, and Tash knew that Mum would have to leave soon too. She didn't want her to go. She was excited about being at ballet school and was trying to tell herself that sleeping in a dormitory would be like being at a sleepover...but a sleepover was with best friends and it was just for one night. This was for weeks and weeks, and she didn't know anyone.

"Come on, Tashie," Mum said gently, calling her by the name she hadn't used since Tash was a little girl. "Time to go."

Tash's dark-brown eyes were filling with tears already. Mum gave her a long hug, and then they went downstairs.

Outside, lots of young dancers were saying goodbye to their families. Tash was almost knocked down by two little dark-haired boys in football kits running in circles round their sister, who was being hugged by both parents at once.

"Sorry," their mum apologized. "Sachin! Ravi! Stop that! Say goodbye to your sister nicely or I'll take away the Xbox."

Tash and Mum smiled at each other and moved out of the way.

"Text me any time you want to talk and I'll get on Skype," said Mum.

Tash nodded and sniffed, blinking back more tears. Mum pulled Tash in for another hug. "You're going to be fine. You've worked so hard to get here and I'm *so* proud of you. Enjoy it. And if you really hate it, you can come home."

"I won't," Tash said, determination rising up

inside her. She was here to become a professional dancer. And she wasn't leaving until it was to start dancing with a ballet company. "I'll be okay."

Mum hugged Tash tightly again, and then she let her go. Tash tried a brave smile, which faded as she watched Mum walk back down the drive towards the car. Tash looked up at the big mansion house that was going to be her home for the next seven years. She felt very small and alone.

Standing back outside her new dormitory, Tash took a deep breath. She felt really nervous now that she was here all by herself. She was about to meet the girls she'd be sharing a room with for the next year; she really hoped they were friendly. She knew that she should just go into the room and meet them, but she was worried that they wouldn't like her or that she wouldn't be able to think of anything funny or interesting to say.

As she hesitated, she noticed a sign on the door, which told her that their room was called

Coppélia. When she felt tears starting to sting her eyes again, she focused on the name. She loved the ballet *Coppélia* because it was so happy and sunny. She thought about the music and the light, bouncy steps of the ballet and felt a bit better. Then she hesitantly pushed the door open with her fingertips.

Instantly she spotted Dani, the girl she'd been sitting near at dinner, perched on the bed next to hers. And on the other side was the girl she'd seen saying goodbye to her family outside. She had black hair tied back in a long plait, and she was sitting on her bed, surrounded by messy piles of jeans, T-shirts and books. She looked up and smiled at Tash.

"Hi!" she said. "Earlier we thought you might not be coming. Which would be crazy. Who would turn down a place at Aurora House, right?"

"That *would* be crazy," grinned Tash. "I was just late. I'm Tash, by the way."

"I'm Anisha," replied the black-haired girl.

She introduced the other girls in the room quickly. Dani smiled widely at Tash, and came over to sit on Anisha's bed. On the other side of the room were Donna, Laura and a Norwegian girl called Toril. Toril had clearly been crying a lot, and Tash realized that moving away to school in a completely different country must be a million times harder than one only a few hours' drive away. Tash looked at the sign on the door and thought about the ballet *Coppélia* again to make her feel better about being far away from home.

"The dormitories are all named after ballet roles," explained Dani, noticing that she was looking at it. "For Year Seven, they're all to do with *Coppélia* or *The Nutcracker*. So the girls are in either Coppélia or Clara. And the boys are in Nutcracker and Franz."

"How come you know so much about the school?" Tash asked.

"My sister's in the Sixth Form," said Dani.

"Ohhhh!" Tash smiled brightly. That explained it!

"I've been here so many times to watch Helen dance in things that most of the teachers know me. They all saw me running around like an idiot in a princess dress and fairy wings when I was five and Helen was in her first year here."

Dani grimaced but her eyes sparkled and Tash could tell she found it funny instead of embarrassing. They both laughed.

"This is so exciting, isn't it?" Anisha gushed suddenly. "Can you believe we're finally here?"

"I still can't believe I got a place!" Tash said with a smile. Soon everyone was sharing stories of how scary the audition had been and how amazed and excited they'd been to be given places at the school. While they talked, they all unpacked their things and put them away in the small wardrobe and chest of drawers next to each bed.

"How terrifying was the bit where we had to talk to Mr Watkins?" said Laura.

"*So* scary!" agreed Donna. "My mind went completely blank when he asked me why I wanted to be a dancer."

"I was way more afraid of messing up the dance part than the talking part," said Dani. "I really thought I was going to forget what steps they'd told us to do and that I'd have to try and copy someone else without making it obvious."

Everyone laughed, but Tash could see from Dani's face that she had been really worried at the time.

"I was frightened to speak English," Toril said quietly and slowly. "I am not good at that."

"But you *are* good," said Laura. "And I'm sure you'll get even better really quickly."

They all nodded at Toril with kind smiles.

"Done!" exclaimed Anisha, after a while. "I thought I'd *never* get all my ballet stuff to fit in that drawer."

Tash smiled at her. She was just about finished, too. She sat down on her bed and carried on chatting with the others until a teacher came in and told them it was time to go to bed.

It was weird being told to go to bed by someone who wasn't Mum. Mum wouldn't be here to give her a kiss goodnight, either. She pulled her phone out of her pocket and sent Mum a quick text: *Bedtime now. Night-night! xx* It wasn't at all the same as saying it in person, but it would have to do.

Half an hour later, they were all in bed, and the darkness made the room feel even stranger. At home, Tash could always see a bright line of light from the landing under her bedroom door. This room was completely dark and Tash could feel the unfamiliar space all around her.

"Tash? Are you awake?" Anisha whispered.

"Yes," Tash whispered back, sitting up. "I can't sleep."

"Me neither," whispered Dani. Tash could hear slow breathing and occasional snores coming from the other side of the room where Donna, Laura and Toril were asleep.

"What do you think tomorrow morning's ballet class will be like?" Anisha asked.

"I can't wait to find out," said Dani. Tash heard her get out of bed and pad across the carpet to the window, where she pulled the curtain back a tiny bit to look outside. A sliver of moonlight lit the dormitory with a dim glow, and Dani pushed the curtain back a little more so that the room wasn't so dark any more. Tash wondered if she felt strange sleeping here too. Dani tiptoed across the room and sat on the end of Tash's bed.

"I've never done a two-hour class before," said Anisha.

She sounded worried but Tash couldn't help a smile at the thought of beginning every day with two hours of her favourite thing in the world.

"I think the first few classes will probably focus on the basics. Make sure we're all doing those perfectly," said Dani. "That's what Helen said anyway. This is her last year here." Her face fell into a frown. "Did I tell you she's one of the best dancers in the school? So it will be great fun when they see what *I'm* like in the studio tomorrow. I'll never be as good as her."

"You'll be great," said Anisha. "You must be good, or they wouldn't have offered you a place."

Dani smiled. "None of us will be very good if we don't sleep," she said, and she tiptoed back to her bed.

Tash lay back down, thinking about Anisha's words in the silent room. She was used to being the best in her ballet class, but tomorrow she'd be just one girl in a class where everyone was good. What if the others were all better than her? Anisha was right, she knew – she must be good enough for the school or they wouldn't have taken her, let alone offered her a scholarship. But the scholarship made her different. Good enough *wasn't* good enough. She had to be *better* than the others. It felt like a challenge – but Tash loved the challenge of learning new ballet steps, and she couldn't wait to see what she could achieve in her first class.

Chapter 3

Tash woke up to the sound of the alarm on her mobile phone. She flung her arm out towards her bedside table but found only empty air. She sat up, confused, and then remembered where she was. Ballet school! The alarm was still going so she quickly turned to the other side of the bed and fumbled with her phone on the shelf next to the headboard. She was wide awake and impatient to get to her first ballet class. The others were getting up, too. They all dressed in the pale pink ballet tights and navy-blue leotards that were the school ballet uniform. Then they pulled on their school zip-up hoodies and tracksuit trousers over their dance clothes, slipped their feet into their school shoes, and went down to the dining room for breakfast.

Tash had been worried about finding it again, but it was easy to follow the crowds of girls and boys all heading the same way. There was a big choice of different fruit, cereals and toast, so she filled a bowl with cornflakes and milk, and took a banana for afterwards. She wanted to make sure she ate enough to have the energy for two hours' dancing, but she didn't want to get a stitch in the middle of it! The six girls from Coppélia found space at a table and ate together, all of them looking around at the older students, who even seemed to sit at tables with the grace of dancers.

After breakfast they had twenty minutes to make their beds, brush their teeth and put their hair up into buns. Tash had put her long, dark hair in a ponytail before they went down for breakfast and it didn't take her very long to twist it up into a bun. She'd been doing her own hair for ballet for about a year. It had been really difficult at first, but by now she knew exactly where she needed to put the pins to hold the bun in place and her fingers got the job done automatically. She watched the others trying to share the mirror while she made her bed, and she was glad her hair wasn't as long and thick as Anisha's. Her new friend still hadn't mastered putting it up by herself and Dani had to help her push the pins in.

"I wonder what Miss Anderbel will be like as our ballet teacher…" said Dani, when they were on their way across the school grounds to the ballet studios. A path led from the main school building to the newer block, which housed eight dance studios as well as changing rooms, a music room and a rest area with sofas and space for stretching out between classes. "She's always been really nice when I've spoken to her, but Helen said she can be really demanding in class!"

"Just think, she used to be a principal dancer at City Ballet!" said Tash.

"And we get to be taught by her!" squealed Anisha.

Ten minutes later, the three of them were standing with the other nine girls in their year at the *barre* in one of the smaller studios. The boys had separate classes because they did different exercises to the girls. Tash felt fidgety standing with one hand resting on the smooth wooden *barre* in her new blue leotard and her soft ballet shoes. They were perfect pink now but *that* wouldn't last long. With four hours of dancing a day – two before academic lessons and two after them – everyone's ballet shoes were going to get worn out very, very quickly.

Tash couldn't wait to get started, but she was also nervous. She was about to dance with her new ballet class for the first time, and she'd soon find out just how good her classmates were. More than that, she wanted to show Miss Anderbel that she was good too.

Tash had expected her first class at Aurora House to be weird and difficult because it would surely be so different to her lessons in the church hall at home. It *was* different – the bright studio with big mirrors, the *barre*s attached to the walls and the lovely smooth floor with no sticky or broken patches were worlds away from what she was used to – but it was also somehow the same. They did the same exercises she'd done in her classes at home, in the same order. They had different sequences and patterns because Miss Anderbel made them up herself, but when they'd done *pliés* first and followed them with *tendus*, Tash knew to expect *battements glisses* next.

Before each exercise, Miss Anderbel talked them through the steps and demonstrated what they should look like. At first Tash couldn't understand why. They had all got places at Aurora

House, so couldn't they all do these steps already? But she soon realized, like Dani had said, that Miss Anderbel wanted to make sure they were all performing the exercises absolutely correctly, and that the teacher was very good at spotting even the tiniest mistake. She was kind and encouraging as well as strict on technique, and when she demonstrated some of the steps she was as graceful as if she was dancing the role of Odette, the white swan in *Swan Lake*.

Tash listened carefully to everything she said and quickly tried the steps facing the mirror so that she could check what all the different parts of her body were doing. Miss Anderbel walked up and down by the *barres* as they danced, correcting people here and there, and Tash listened carefully to those things too, determined to get everything right. She already liked Miss Anderbel and she really wanted to impress her.

After a while, the pressure of dancing at her new school for the first time melted away. Tash's mind was busy making sure that she remembered to keep her back straight, to turn out properly, to stretch her legs, and to keep her shoulders down and her eyes up. There were so many little things that added up to create a graceful dancer, and Tash loved it all. She felt like she was taken out of the real world during class and transported to a place where the only thing that mattered was the feeling of movement combining beautifully with music.

"Use the floor," Miss Anderbel said to Anisha when they were doing *grands battements*. "Try to really push your foot against the floor as you bring your leg forward."

Even though the correction wasn't for her, Tash thought about the teacher's words as she moved her leg out to the side, trying to make sure she was really using the floor too.

"Good, Tash." Miss Anderbel smiled as she walked past.

Tash bit back a little grin and carried on with

the exercise, but inside she was bouncing. She wasn't even halfway through her first class and she'd already been praised!

"Look out towards your audience, Dani," Miss Anderbel said later, when they were doing *port de bras* in the centre. "Don't look down at the floor."

The exercise name meant "movement of the arms" – Tash's old ballet teacher had been obsessed with making them learn what all the French names for steps meant – so the exercises were usually done standing in one place and only moving the arms, head and upper body.

Tash was already looking out at the "audience", which was just the mirror at the front of the studio, but she made doubly sure that she was putting a lot of expression into the way she moved her head and arms. She adored exercises like this, where she could imagine that she was dancing in *Swan Lake* or *The Sleeping Beauty* and that she was gesturing out to an audience of hundreds of people instead of just her own reflection.

"That was *lovely*, Tash," Miss Anderbel said at the end of the exercise. "We don't have time to repeat that exercise, but tomorrow I want all of you to really present it to me. Just because you're not moving your legs, it doesn't mean you're not dancing."

Tash went red at being singled out like that again, but she was thrilled at the praise.

They danced through the rest of the class with a lovely slow exercise full of *arabesques* and graceful turns, and some quick sequences of small bouncy jumps. They did these exercises in two groups, so Tash got a chance to properly watch some of her classmates dance for the first time. Every single one of them was good. Tash had expected that, but actually seeing it felt different. She knew that she was the only one who was here on a scholarship because the school only offered two every year – one for girls and one for boys. She had a lot to live up to!

"Try to jump higher, Tash," Miss Anderbel said to her, when they were doing *sissonnes* diagonally across the room. The jump started in fifth position, and as she jumped up, she also jumped forward, her back leg flying out straight behind her so that it was almost like doing an *arabesque* in the air. "Use your *plié* to push yourself off the floor."

Tash nodded and tried harder, but inside she was annoyed with herself. It was embarrassing to be reminded about something so easy; Miss Anderbel hadn't had to tell anyone else to use their *pliés* to get higher in the air.

She promised herself she'd work much harder on jumps – she was going to show Miss Anderbel that she was here to learn, that she was here to become a perfect ballerina and that she truly deserved the scholarship the school had given her. She was determined not to let them down.

Chapter 4

After their ballet class, Tash and her new friends only had twenty minutes to change out of their leotards and tights into their school uniform and to have a drink and a piece of fruit from the box that was provided every day in the rest area. The Year Eight and Nine girls were also using the changing room in the studio block to change from dance to school clothes, so it was a frantic mad crush by the time Tash had found a space for herself and untied the ribbons on her ballet shoes. On Dani's suggestion – another handy tip from Helen – the girls in Coppélia dorm had all brought small towels with them to the studio along with their grey school skirts, white shirts and navy-blue jumpers that matched the colour of the school leotard. Tash hurriedly scrubbed off the sweat from dancing, sprayed herself with body spray (by this time the changing room smelled strongly of a strange mixture of all the different body sprays the girls had brought with them) and struggled into her school uniform. It was uncomfortable when she was so hot and the frantic race against time didn't help.

"Ready?" asked Anisha, squeezing through into a space between Tash and Dani.

She was somehow already dressed and had her bag containing her dance clothes and pencil case slung over her shoulder.

"Hang on," pleaded Dani, who was hopping around trying to put her shoes on and do up the buttons on her shirt at the same time.

The Year Eights and Nines, who'd had lots of practice at the quick change, had mostly gone to their classrooms already. Tash swept her leotard and tights into her bag.

"Ready!" she said with a smile.

She looked at her watch. They still had five minutes to get to their form room before academic school started. When Dani was ready, the three girls half-ran back to the main building, grabbing an apple each on their way through the rest area. They hadn't had time to do anything to their hair; Tash hoped that she didn't get told off about the wisps of hair flying out from the bun that had started the morning so neatly.

The others had all been shown the way to their form room the previous afternoon, while Tash and Mum were still stuck in traffic. Between them, Dani and Anisha managed to remember how to get there and they arrived at their form room along with the other girls in their class, to find that most of the boys were already there. They'd obviously managed to get changed a lot faster. Tash noticed that hardly any of the girls had been able to tidy their hair and most of them looked a bit red in the face and uncomfortable from the mad rush between classes. It was clear that, as well as practising ballet steps, they would all have to practise rapid changes – good training for a life in the theatre!

Tash and Anisha sat down together at one of the tables, and Dani took the seat behind them next to Toril. Everyone was talking about the ballet class they'd just done when a tall man came into the room.

"Are we all here?" he asked. "I think I met most of you last night, but in case you've forgotten your boring old form teacher in the excitement of your first ballet class, I'll introduce myself again. I'm Mr Kent and I'll be teaching you English and drama. Usually you'll have two academic lessons before lunch. As it's your first day, we'll use the first one to go through your timetable and sort out homework diaries, and then you'll go to your second lesson. But before we get stuck into all that, let's get to know each other a bit better. I want all of you to pair up with someone you haven't spoken to yet. Yes, Rob," he said, noticing one of the boys looking worried, "that means you're going to have to talk to a *girl*!"

His voice got high-pitched and silly at the end of the sentence and the entire class giggled.

"Wait, wait, wait!" he called as the class started getting up to change places. "There are some rules. Number one, talk to someone you haven't spoken to before. Number two, and this is the bit you're all going to find *extremely* difficult...no ballet talk! There'll be loads of time for that, so right now I want you to talk about the other things you're interested in. I'm sure you'll be able to think of at least *one* other topic. Find a partner and then you've got five minutes until we switch around again!"

Tash's first partner was Rob, who was still bright red from being singled out by Mr Kent, and they talked about their favourite TV shows (*Strictly Come Dancing* and *Junior Bake Off* for both of them). Then she found herself next to a girl from Clara dorm called Lily-May. Only ten minutes into that morning's ballet class, Tash had noticed that Lily-May was one of the best dancers there. She had golden hair, which had somehow stayed neat and tidy throughout the class, and her bright-blue eyes were filled with the total confidence of a girl who knew she was talented. But talking to each other when ballet was a banned topic turned out to be really difficult. Lily-May didn't watch much TV, and she and Tash didn't like any of the same pop music. In the end, they landed on summer holidays, but even that didn't work because it seemed as if the only thing Lily-May had done was attend the City Ballet junior classes, and they weren't allowed to talk about that. Tash sighed.

"Time's up!" called Mr Kent, saving Tash from their non-conversation. "Move along, please, ladies and gentlemen," he added in a funny voice that sounded like an old-fashioned train conductor Tash had seen in a film once. Tash ended up next to a small boy with curly black hair.

"I'm Jonah," he said, and then grinned. "I've found a way around the rules. Want to know?" Tash nodded. "Mr Kent didn't say no talking about *dance*, right? Just ballet. So, what other kinds of dance have you done?"

Tash laughed, and the conversation took off from there. They'd both done tap and a bit of contemporary, and Jonah had also done years of street dance before he started ballet. Tash didn't think she'd ever met anyone so enthusiastic. She thought about Mr Kent's no-ballet-talk rule and smiled to herself. It was amazing to be in a classroom where that rule was needed!

Mr Kent handed out timetables and homework diaries, and then he talked them through the general school rules.

"I'm sure most of them won't need any explanation. No running in the corridors – we don't want any injuries! You must be on time for all your classes, as well as meals and your supervised homework time."

Tash listened, thinking that the rules were pretty much the same as the rules at her junior school had been. But Aurora House was a boarding school, so of course there were rules for their free time, too.

"You're not allowed to go into town without a teacher or an older student until you're in Year Ten," Mr Kent continued. "And until then, you can't use the dance studios outside of your classes either, unless you have a teacher for supervision. Four hours of dancing a day should be enough for all of you, anyway – we don't want our youngest students burning out!"

Tash pulled a face at Dani. That last rule didn't make much sense to her, and the reason Mr Kent gave seemed silly. They were all here to become ballet dancers – there was no chance they'd practise too much and get sick of it!

But there wasn't time to talk about it because moments later they were on their way to their first real lesson: history. Tash was thrilled when Miss Dixon told them that they'd be learning about the history of ballet as well as the things people learned about at normal schools. Tash had loads of ballet books and DVDs, but she was excited about finding out more. It was so cool that ballet was a proper school subject here.

After eating spaghetti bolognese for lunch in the dining room with the rest of the school, Tash, Dani and Anisha went outside to explore. The school grounds were massive and they knew there must be loads to discover. They chatted while they wandered across the grass, going over every detail of the ballet class, and then laughing about the hour with Mr Kent.

"Did you talk to Lily-May?" Tash asked the others.

"Yeah," said Dani, pulling a face that showed exactly what she thought of her.

"She's an amazing dancer," said Anisha.

"And she knows it," said Dani.

Tash and Dani shared a smile.

"Her face when Miss Anderbel praised you was hilarious, Tash," said Anisha.

"I didn't see," said Tash.

"*Your* face was pretty hilarious, too," Dani said to Tash. "You looked like you'd never been so shocked in your life!"

"I *was* shocked," laughed Tash.

"You shouldn't be," said Dani. "You're really good."

"So are you two," replied Tash. "Both of you are better at jumps than me."

"We're all good," agreed Anisha. "We wouldn't be here otherwise."

"So wise!" said Dani. "Oh hey, this is really pretty!"

Tash looked up and found that they were in the middle of a clump of apple trees. The September sunshine dappled the leaves, and green apples hung from the branches. Birds cheeped in the sky and in the highest branches of the trees. The grass was dry so they sat down for a while and Tash leaned back on her hands, staring up at the shapes of blue sky that she could see through the gaps in the leaves. They still had another two hours of school and then another two-hour dance class – contemporary this time. She was already tired. But she was so, *so* happy.

Chapter 5

Life at Aurora House was better than Tash had ever dreamed. She'd known that she'd get to dance every day and she'd imagined that the other girls and boys would love dancing as much as she did, but she'd had no idea what it would feel like to be a real ballet student at a serious ballet school. It wasn't just her own life that revolved around ballet any more; here, ballet was the centre of everybody's world.

Every morning began with two hours of ballet and then the mad rush to be ready for their pens-and-paper lessons. Year Seven's teachers had trouble getting them to focus on anything but ballet; whether they were sitting in a maths lesson or doing a science experiment, before ten minutes had passed someone would start talking about that morning's dance class, and anyone sitting near them would join in. Mr Kent's ballet-talk ban was enforced for every English and drama lesson, but even he couldn't always keep the excited young dancers from comparing notes on how difficult the exercises had been and who had performed them best.

Academic lessons finished at 3.15 p.m. and then they had half an hour to change back into leotards and have a snack before their second dose of dance. The afternoon class wasn't the same every day; twice a week they had contemporary dance, another two days were character dance, at which Anisha excelled, and on Fridays they were taught the very basics of *pas de deux* – the art of dancing as partners. As they moved up the school and gained strength and technique, Tash knew this class would become more and more important.

For now, though, the main point of *pas de deux* was learning to work with a partner. In the first class, Tash was paired up with a boy called Nick, while Anisha was with a quiet, blond boy named Will and tiny Dani ended up with Jonah because she was the only girl smaller than him. She gave Tash a grin. The night before, the Coppélia girls had laid in bed after lights-out talking about the *pas de deux* class the next day and wondering who their partners would be. All six of them had wanted to be paired up with Jonah because they'd all thought he'd be the most fun. He was already getting a reputation for his cheeky jokes and enthusiasm, and even though he was the smallest boy in the year, Tash had heard from the others that he was by far the best in their class at *pirouettes* and other turns.

Perfect Pirouette

When they were all paired up, Mr Edwards, their teacher, began to teach them the steps for a short dance. He was very tall and strode around the studio as if he was onstage, calling instructions in his booming voice. There was giggling all around the room when he asked them to hold hands with their partners, and a lot of people went bright red. The boys had to hold out one arm to the front while the girls stepped up into an *arabesque* on *demi-pointe*, taking their partner's hand for balance and raising their other arm to fifth above their heads. Tash was a bit embarrassed too, but holding hands was part of the mechanics of doing the step, no different from "spotting" during a *pirouette* to stop from getting dizzy; it didn't *mean* anything. Anyway, once they really got into the dancing, Tash forgot all about how weird it was; with Nick's hand for balance, she felt as if she could hold her *arabesque* for ever and ever. She felt strong, like a real ballerina. It was amazing.

"Very nice," Mr Edwards said to Tash and Nick after they'd performed the exercise in a small group at the end of the class. "But, Tash, when you turn in your *pirouettes*, make sure you're really holding your core, your stomach muscles. If you don't, it'll be harder for you to stay up and do lots of turns."

Tash felt as if all the joy that came from dancing had just been knocked out of her. She'd already found out she wasn't the best at jumps, and now she wasn't the best at turning either. Ballet had always been what she thought about before she went to sleep, while she got dressed in the mornings and when she daydreamed in lessons at her junior school. Being a dancer was such a huge part of who she was that sometimes she wondered how other people lived without it. She knew that only the most talented students would get to be dancers at City Ballet when they left school, and she was determined to be one of them. It mattered to her more than anything, and being criticized by her teachers on simple jumps and single *pirouettes* made her feel as if the dream was already slipping out of reach.

She'd been the best dancer in her ballet class at home, so she'd come to Aurora House aiming to be the best here, too. But it looked as if she had a long way to go. She was starting to wonder if the teachers had chosen the right person when they'd given the scholarship to her, and she was worried that they might be thinking the same thing.

She leaned against the *barre* at the side of the room to watch the second group perform. Anisha and Will were in this group, and Tash started watching them, but her eyes were drawn almost immediately to Lily-May and Rob, dancing at the front of the studio. Everything they did was perfect. It didn't seem possible that they'd learned the steps only two hours ago.

Since she'd started at Aurora House, Tash had been having a wonderful time, but every now and then she was reminded that the ballet world was incredibly competitive. Watching Lily-May, she felt the dream of perfection pulling at her, urging her to work harder.

At the end of the class, while the others filed out to the changing room, Tash found a space in front of one of the mirrors and tried a *pirouette*. It was hard to watch herself while turning, but she focused on what Mr Edwards had said, and she could feel that he was right. She tried again, putting all her concentration into holding her core muscles and keeping her upper body steady.

"That's it!" cried Mr Edwards, surprising Tash, who hadn't known she was being watched. "Now show me a double."

Tash did as she was told and performed a double *pirouette*, but she could feel that it wasn't right. She pulled a face as she came out of it and didn't wait for Mr Edwards to say anything before trying again. This one was better.

"Good," he said. "I want to see that every time now."

Tash grinned and bounced out of the studio. There was no feeling in the world like doing a ballet step well.

"What were you doing?" asked Dani, who was already changed back into school uniform.

"Sorting out my *pirouettes*," said Tash, crashing out on the bench for a moment. They had thirty minutes until dinner, so she knew she could take her time.

"They're fine," said Anisha. "They're better than mine."

"But they're not *perfect*," insisted Tash.

Anisha shrugged. "We've got loads of time for that," she said. "I'm so tired, I don't think I could even do a quarter of a turn right now!"

Tash laughed. "Good thing you don't have to do *any* turns until Monday!"

"It's the weekend!" cried Dani, and pretended to collapse on the bench next to Tash, who was pulling her school skirt on while sitting down. She suddenly felt like she'd never been so tired in her life.

Dinner gave more energy to all of them, though. Most days, they had an hour of supervised homework time after they'd eaten, but on Fridays they had free time instead and as it was still warm outside, Year Seven spent the fading twilight in a laughing, shrieking game of tag.

"Tag!" cried Dani, stretching out an arm and catching Tash by the shoulder as she tried to run away.

Tash stopped running and gasped in air, turning around to see if she could find an easy target to tag. Dani had already skipped away, so Tash ran for Anisha who had slowed down and was chatting to Jonah. They saw Tash coming and split apart, running in opposite directions. Tash hesitated, darting from one side to the other, and eventually sprinted after Anisha.

"Caught you!" she shouted as she tagged Anisha.

They were both running too fast to stop and collided with Dani, the three of them falling to the ground. They lay there for a moment, catching their breath.

"Tag," said Anisha, tapping Tash's arm.

"Tag," Tash replied, tapping Anisha back.

They giggled. Tash thought she could happily lie here for ever with her new friends, tired out from dancing and playing games.

The game went on until no one could run any more and the sky had turned a peaceful inky blue. Then they all went back inside, laughing and talking all the way, high on the thought that they'd made it through their first week of ballet school, and excited that they had so many more to come.

Tash's first full week of dancing had passed in a blur and it was only now, with the weekend just beginning, that she had time to take a breath and realize that she really missed Mum. She chatted with her on Skype on Saturday afternoon, in the empty Coppélia dorm, and told her everything about life at Aurora House.

"It's *so* cool, Mum, the studios are amazing and we get to do four hours of dancing every day!"

"It sounds like you're having a great time," said Mum.

"I miss you a lot," said Tash.

She *was* enjoying ballet school, but everything still felt so new that it was hard to imagine staying for weeks and weeks before going home. Talking to Mum made her remember that she was going to be here for a long time. It was an overwhelming thought.

"I miss you too," said Mum. And then, obviously hoping to distract Tash from her worries, she changed the subject. "What are the other girls in your class like?"

"They're nice," Tash said. "I've made friends with the girls in my dormitory. Especially Dani and Anisha, they're so much fun. Everyone here is a *really* good dancer."

She looked down at the keyboard of her laptop and fiddled with some of the keys.

"Of course they are, it's a difficult school to get into," said Mum. "But *you're* a really good dancer, too."

Tash smiled, looking back up at Mum.

"How are your school lessons?"

"They're okay," said Tash. "We get to learn about the history of ballet!"

"I bet you're already coming top of that class," laughed Mum.

Tash laughed too. She *had* done well in her first history lesson, because it was so interesting, but that wasn't the class that she cared about being the best in.

After speaking to Mum, Tash didn't really know what to do. She wished they could have kept on talking all day. She, Dani and Anisha had finished off their homework together that morning in their form room, where they had homework time every Saturday morning, supervised by Mr Kent. She wandered into the Year Seven and Eight common room where some of the others were watching TV. She joined them for a while, but she felt restless and her mind kept going back to Mr Edwards' correction in the *pas de deux* class. She was longing to work more on her *pirouettes*. It had felt so good doing a double just the way it should be, and she had a feeling that her turns would be much better and much easier to do once she'd trained herself to hold her core muscles automatically. She went back up to Coppélia and found Dani and Anisha sitting on Anisha's bed looking at a magazine.

"Do you guys want to go over that *pirouettes* exercise we did the other day?" Tash asked them.

"No way," said Anisha. "I don't want to use my feet *at all* today!"

"Sorry," said Dani. "I'm talking to my parents on Skype in ten minutes."

"Just a suggestion," Tash said with a smile. "I think I'll have a quick go."

She put her ballet shoes on over her socks and did the exercise a few times in the middle of the room, trying to really focus on doing the *pirouettes* as tidily as possible. But it wasn't easy on the carpeted floor, and her skinny jeans made it difficult to bend her knees fully and get her lifted foot into the right position. After a while she gave up and went to sit on the bed with her friends. They moved the magazine over a bit so that she could see, and Tash tried to read the problem page they were giggling at, but she couldn't focus on it properly. Her mind was so busy with missing Mum, and worrying about the scholarship and her dancing, that there wasn't room for anything else. She didn't understand how Anisha and Dani could switch all that off so easily. But then she realized: they didn't have to worry about losing a scholarship.

They all had the same love for ballet, but Tash knew that she was still different.

She worried on and off all weekend, and most of the next week, too. She tried practising *pirouettes* in the dormitory and in the common room and she did *pliés* holding on to the sink with one hand while she brushed her teeth, but it was impossible to practise properly in any of those places. She wished she could stay behind in the studio after the morning classes and work on her *pirouettes* by herself, but there was always English or maths or history to rush off to.

"Stop, stop!" Miss Anderbel called out in the middle of a *pirouettes* exercise during Thursday morning's ballet class. "Tash, your upper body is all over the place. What do you think will happen if you try a double *pirouette* like that?"

"It'll throw me off balance," Tash responded in a quiet voice.

"Exactly," said Miss Anderbel. "Really pay attention to that. It's so important."

Tash listened carefully to Miss Anderbel and tried again, desperate to show her teacher that she could do better. She *knew* she could; she'd shown Mr Edwards that she understood his correction and she was angry with herself for making the same mistake again. She'd been worrying so much about whether or not her *grands battements* at the *barre* had been high enough that she'd forgotten to focus on the very thing she needed to work on!

"Better," said Miss Anderbel. "Now do that in the exercise, please. From the beginning, everyone!"

The whole class went back to the starting position, standing in fifth position with their arms curved low in front of them, facing the mirrors. Tash focused really hard on a spot where two of the mirrors joined. She knew that Miss Anderbel was only trying to help her improve, but having her stop the exercise to explain to her how to do a *pirouette* was really embarrassing.

Being singled out for doing something well had made Tash feel like she was floating up to the studio's high ceiling; being singled out because she was doing something badly felt like being crushed into the floor.

* * *

That evening, after dinner and homework, Tash made a decision. She gathered her ballet shoes and a T-shirt and leggings and headed back over to the studios. Halfway down the path, she hesitated. She was breaking the school rules. The Year Seven, Eight and Nine students were not allowed to use the studios outside of their classes.

Tash didn't *want* to do anything wrong or get into trouble, especially when she was still so new at the school, but she couldn't face another class with Miss Anderbel until her *pirouettes* were better. She wondered if she should run back to the common room and persuade Dani or Anisha to come with her. But she didn't want to get them into trouble. And although she wanted to tell them what she was doing, she was ashamed that she was having trouble with *pirouettes*, something they could both do well, and she was worried they wouldn't understand how much she *needed* to do this.

Perfect Pirouette

Talking to her teachers about her worries was out of the question too. More than anything, she was afraid that if they knew she already needed extra practice they'd realize they'd made the wrong choice.

So she looked determinedly ahead of her and walked through the door into the studio block before she could change her mind. She was only going to do it once, she told herself, just to get her *pirouettes* right. She tried to convince herself that that made it okay.

The ballet studio was empty and peaceful. Moonlight streamed in brightly through the high window, until Tash flicked the lights on and ruined the beautiful patterns on the floor. Fairy-tale lighting was the stuff of the stage; Tash had come to the studio to work hard. She warmed her muscles up at the *barre* and then did *pirouette* after *pirouette* until she was pleased with the way they felt – she held her upper body steady, just as

Mr Edwards had taught her, and she finished each turn neatly and precisely.

Tash glanced at the clock on the wall. She'd been here for an hour and it would soon be time for bed. One more. She pointed her foot out to the side and closed it behind her in a fourth position *plié*, the preparation position she liked best. She focused on a spot where two mirrors joined, then spun round in a *pirouette* – once, twice, *three times*! – whipping her head round each time to focus on the same spot. She finished neatly in fifth position, and then jumped wildly into the air in delight. Tash had never done a good triple *pirouette* before. She couldn't wait to tell Dani and Anisha.

Then she remembered – no one knew she'd been doing extra practice. She realized she liked having the studio to herself and being able to really *feel* her own dancing without anyone else there. Practising ballet was so addictive that she already wanted to come to the studio by herself again, but if she wanted to keep doing this, she'd have to carry on keeping it secret from her friends. Otherwise they'd probably try to persuade her not to break the rules again or, if she brought them in on it, there was a chance that they might get in trouble, too. The idea of lying to Dani and Anisha didn't feel very good. But extra practice would make her a better dancer…and maybe she'd only need to do a couple more sessions, just enough to make her *pirouettes* consistently brilliant so that she could do them perfectly every time. Then one day soon she'd surprise everyone with an amazing triple in morning class.

She remembered the feeling she'd just had while spinning around and all of her worries faded away, replaced by a love of ballet that was so strong she felt as if her limbs couldn't possibly contain it. She danced all the way down the path and up the stairs to Coppélia. And when she fell asleep, she dreamed of dancing *Swan Lake* all night long.

Chapter 6

Tash settled into the routine of Aurora House almost without realizing it – getting up early and dashing in and out of the bathroom so that her friends would have time to use it too, dancing and studying, more dancing and homework, evenings playing noisy games in the common room with the rest of her year, and whispered chats in the dark with Dani and Anisha in the few minutes after lights-out.

Perfect Pirouette

They learned traditional dance styles from other countries in their character dance classes, and moved in new ways in contemporary classes. Mr Edwards taught them a simple *pas de deux* piece, which they worked on week after week, concentrating on acting the steps in the style of different characters and moods as well as dancing them. Anisha was by far the best at the acting side of things, and she amazed everyone by making the same steps look completely different if she was pretending to be happy, sad, angry or comical.

Every now and then, people fell out over a missing book or argued over what to watch on TV and gossip would ripple rapidly through the class until they made friends again; the Coppélia girls took to hiding under their beds in fits of giggles when Miss Dixon, the head of Year Seven and Eight as well as their history teacher, came to say goodnight to them; everyone stressed out when a maths test rolled around but then ran away from their worries in an epic lunchtime game of Stuck in the Mud. The days flew by and danced Tash along with them.

"I can't believe we've been here six weeks already," said Anisha one Friday evening while they sat in the common room.

Dani was painting Tash's nails with shimmery pink nail varnish. They could hear *The Simpsons* on the TV on the other side of the room and some of the Year Eights were playing a crashing, laughing game of Jenga.

"It's gone so fast," agreed Dani.

"But I also feel like I've lived here for ever," said Tash.

"Done!" said Dani, screwing the lid back onto the little bottle of nail varnish. "Your turn, Anisha. Pick a colour."

Tash placed her hands carefully on her knees so that she didn't smudge the nail varnish – even though she'd knew she'd have to take it off before school on Monday – and leaned back against the wall. They were all sitting cross-legged on the floor in a corner, and Tash watched the Jenga game and the people in front of the TV, and others who were reading and chatting and using their laptops to send emails or play games or watch films. She was getting to know everyone in her year and the year above, finding out what made them laugh and what annoyed them, what music they liked, which TV shows were their favourites and what they talked about when they weren't talking about ballet. Being at school together, dancing together and sharing a bedroom had already helped her to feel closer to Dani and Anisha than she'd ever felt to Maddy, even after four years of being friends at junior school.

As Tash waited for her nail varnish to dry, she thought about the ballet exercise she intended to try in her next secret practice session. At first she'd only planned to use the studio by herself just once, just to get her *pirouettes* right, but she couldn't seem to stop herself going back again and again. It was only once a week, usually on Monday evenings when everyone else was busy relaxing. Every time, she promised herself it would be the last secret practice she did, but she could never help going back. Having space to herself to work on the steps that were bothering her just felt too important. And the more she went back without anyone catching her, the more she began to believe that no one would ever find out.

"Have you planned loads of fun things for half-term?" Dani asked, interrupting Tash's thoughts.

Tash looked at her, confused.

"We've only got another week of school left before we have a week off!" Dani reminded her.

Tash realized she was right – she couldn't believe it had come around so soon! She couldn't wait to see Mum, relax at home for a week and do all the fun things they'd talked about in emails and phone calls.

That weekend, everyone was starting to compare plans for the short holiday. Most people were going home, but some were staying at school because their homes were too far away or because their parents weren't able to take time off work to be with them. Dani and Anisha were among the small number of Year Sevens who were staying at school, but they were talking about their plans for a week off lessons just as much as the people who were actually getting away from Aurora House. They'd spent ages planning which films to watch when they'd have the common room almost to themselves. Years Seven and Eight weren't allowed to go into town unless they were with some of the older students, so they were also absorbed in trying to persuade Helen to take them shopping.

Tash was dying to see Mum. They would go shopping and watch films, and share lovely autumn walks in their favourite park, which was the best place on earth for crunching leaves, finding conkers and watching ducks on the lake. But she couldn't help feeling a bit envious that she'd be missing out on a week of fun with her friends. She wouldn't trade her week with Mum for *anything*, but part of her worried that she'd come back to find that Dani and Anisha had lots of private jokes about things that had happened during half-term, and she'd feel left out.

On Saturday evenings, Years Seven and Eight gathered in their common room to watch a film, which they took turns choosing. Tash wanted to get a bit of homework done before they started on *Singin' in the Rain* – Anisha's choice – so she was up in Coppélia frantically searching for her maths book, which she *knew* she'd stuffed into her dance bag on the way to the studios after school lessons had finished yesterday. She'd just spotted it under the bed and was reaching out to grab it when her phone rang. Tash looked up, surprised. Mum was meant to call her tomorrow, and Maddy never had any credit so they always talked on Skype or sent emails. Who else could possibly want to phone her?

She scrambled to her feet and grabbed her phone from her bed. It *was* Mum, after all. Tash felt her stomach drop, without knowing why. Mum was calling a day early. Did that mean something was wrong?

"Hi," she answered.

"Hi, Tash," said Mum.

"Is everything okay?" Tash asked.

"Oh, darling, I'm so sorry," said Mum. "I've got some bad news for you."

"What?" squeaked Tash, biting her lip.

"I've got to go to a conference in Switzerland over half-term. I wouldn't go if it wasn't *really* important. I know you've been looking forward to coming home, and I so wanted to see you."

"Oh," Tash said quietly.

She'd grown up with Mum missing sports days and school plays because of her job, and she'd thought she was used to it. But this was different. This wasn't just a hundred-metres race on the school field; this was a whole *week* that

Mum and Tash had planned to spend together.

"I'm so sorry," Mum repeated.

She sounded really upset, and Tash realized that half-term had meant as much to Mum as it had to her.

"I know," said Tash. "Don't worry. Christmas isn't *that* far away…"

But as she spoke she glanced at the City Ballet calendar on the wall and thought about all those days stacking up on top of each other. Suddenly the end of term seemed like the top of a mountain that she'd have to climb.

"I'll make it up to you, I promise," said Mum.

"It'll be fine," said Tash. "Dani and Anisha are staying, too."

"Oh, I'm so glad!" said Mum. "At least you'll have your friends. Promise me you'll have loads of fun, okay?"

"Okay," said Tash. "I miss you."

"I miss you too, sweetheart. I'll see if I can come up one weekend and take you out."

"Okay," said Tash, trying hard not to cry. She didn't want Mum to hear it in her voice and get even more upset.

They talked for a little while longer about all the things they'd done during the week – Tash's ballet classes, and Mum's dinner with Maddy's parents and news from Tash's home town. When they said goodbye and Mum finally hung up, Tash dropped her phone onto her bed. She sat down heavily and stared at the wall until tears filled her eyes and dropped onto her cheeks.

By the time Tash had stopped crying and gone down to the common room, the film had already started. Dani had saved a spot and a cushion for her on the floor against one of the walls and she gratefully sank down and crossed her legs. She hoped no one would notice her puffy eyes – an obvious sign that she had been crying. But Dani did.

"You okay?" she whispered.

She looked really worried and Tash almost cried again knowing that her friend cared about her.

"I'm staying for half-term," Tash whispered back.

Dani didn't say anything, but she put her arm around Tash and gave her a sideways hug.

"What's up?" asked Anisha, leaning round from Dani's other side.

"Tash is joining our half-term films and shopping club," said Dani.

"I hope you like Monopoly," grinned Anisha. "We're planning to have an epic game."

"*Anisha's* planning an epic game," retorted Dani. "I think we should play something that *doesn't* last for ever!"

Tash smiled at them both. She was still sad that she wouldn't get to see Mum but at least she had her friends here to cheer her up.

The first day of half-term was bright and almost warm. The grounds of the school were falling under autumn's spell, and the little clump of apple trees had turned a fiery orange. Tash, Dani and Anisha took their school books outside and did the small amount of half-term homework they'd been set sitting under the trees. Tash stretched her legs out on the grass. This was the first Monday morning that hadn't started with a ballet class in a really long time and every part of her was itching to dance. They chatted while they worked, and even though it was only the beginning of half-term, they couldn't help talking about what would happen when school started again next week.

"We'll probably start rehearsing for the Christmas fair," said Dani knowledgeably.

"Rehearsing?" asked Anisha and Tash.

"Each year performs a short piece for parents and other people who've come to the fair," Dani explained. "It's just a normal school fair with stalls and games and stuff. The ballet performances are like when the school choir sings Christmas carols or something."

"Except here, they'll make us rehearse every day for weeks until it's professional standard," laughed Anisha.

"Exactly!" said Dani.

"About time we got to perform something!" cried Anisha. "We work so hard and no one even gets to see us dance, except our teachers."

"Don't worry, Anisha," said Tash. "One day *everyone* will watch you dance. That's why we're here."

They spent the rest of the day relaxing outside. After dinner, everyone gathered in the Sixth-Form common room for a special announcement. Tash, Dani, Anisha and Toril, the only Year Sevens who had stayed, hung shyly at the back of the room while Miss Anderbel waited for everyone to arrive.

"I know that most of you would have preferred to go home this week," said the teacher.

Tash forced herself not to think about what she

and Mum might have been doing at home right now – probably cooking dinner together and then watching one of their favourite films afterwards, saying half of the lines along with the characters on screen.

"So we've organized a special treat for you, to make up for having to spend the week at school," Miss Anderbel went on. "We've managed to get tickets for all of you to see City Ballet perform *The Sleeping Beauty* on Thursday."

A gasp of excitement rushed around the room and everyone started talking at once and showering Miss Anderbel with questions.

"Calm down," laughed Miss Anderbel. "I don't need to remind you that you'll be representing the school and we expect extremely good behaviour. It's very kind of City Ballet to give us these tickets, and I hope you'll all use the performance as inspiration for your own dancing."

Tash and her friends went back to their common room buzzing with the news. The four of them and the three Year Eight boys who'd stayed for half-term all danced around the room ecstatically for a while. Then they hunted around in the DVD collection for *The Sleeping Beauty*, which they watched for the rest of the evening, exclaiming every few seconds about how lucky they were.

They spent the next two days relaxing, watching TV and films, and playing games in the common room. Tash made sure they always included Toril in everything they did. Laura, her best friend at the school, had gone home for the week and Tash knew that Toril must feel very far away from her parents in Norway.

On Wednesday evening they were so excited about the ballet the next day that they couldn't sit still enough to watch a film. Anisha got out the Monopoly board that she'd been threatening them with for days and they groaned at how long a game would take, but as soon as they started playing they were all out to win and having a great time.

"I've always wanted to dance the Lilac Fairy role," admitted Tash while Anisha agonized over whether or not to buy Oxford Street.

"Not the Rose Adagio?" asked Dani, mentioning Aurora's dance, one of the most difficult in all of classical ballet. "That's what I want to do."

"And me," said Toril, twirling one of the little plastic houses around in her fingers and staring dreamily into the distance.

"Well, obviously that too," said Tash with a big smile. "But I think the Lilac Fairy's solo is lovely."

"I think Carabosse the wicked fairy looks fun," said Anisha.

"You would," Dani teased. They'd already discovered Anisha's love of roles that required a lot of acting.

They still hadn't finished their game when it was time to go to bed, so Anisha wrote a note on a piece of paper – *DON'T TOUCH ANYTHING, OR ELSE!!!* – and they left it in the middle of the board, before running up to Coppélia dorm to fall asleep and dream about dancing in *The Sleeping Beauty*.

The next evening, they had fun getting dressed up to go to the theatre. They'd spent all afternoon talking about what to wear and who would sit next to who and what the ballet would be like. Tash chose a dark green dress with white dots and short lacy sleeves, and she brushed her long hair and let it hang down her back. Anisha wore a skirt and a jumper and she tied her hair back into a plait because she hated having it down and in the way. And Dani, after taking everything out of her wardrobe and piling it all on the bed, settled at the last minute on a pink dress. She left her hair loose, too, and Tash realized that she'd hardly ever seen Dani's hair out of a ponytail or bun. Wearing it down made Dani look a lot more dressed up than normal.

"I can't wait to get to the theatre!" said Tash, looking at her watch for the hundredth time that day.

Toril was hunting under her bed for one of her shoes and while they waited for her, Tash, Dani and Anisha stood side by side and looked at themselves in the mirror.

"The others are going to be *so* jealous when they come back after half-term!" said Anisha.

Suddenly Tash was so excited about the ballet that she hugged them both and they all jumped around in a squashed circle until Toril said she was ready.

They went to the theatre on a school coach. The older students headed straight for the seats at the back, so Tash sat next to Anisha near the front, with Dani and Toril in the seats behind them. Miss Anderbel was sitting across the aisle from them and they spent ages asking her questions about what it had been like to dance with City Ballet and which roles she'd liked best.

"I always loved dancing in *Swan Lake*," Miss Anderbel told them. "And City Ballet is a great company to be part of."

"I want to dance with City Ballet when I'm older," said Tash.

"If you continue to work hard, there's no reason why you can't make that happen," said Miss Anderbel. "You've been improving a lot in the last few weeks."

Tash smiled but she felt a bit uneasy. Miss Anderbel had no idea that Tash was doing more dance practice than just her morning and afternoon classes.

When they arrived, Miss Anderbel counted everyone coming off the coach.

"I've got our tickets, so follow me," she said. Then she led them through the main doors into the lobby of the theatre, and over the plush blue carpet towards the attendant standing at the door to the auditorium.

Tash walked along with the others, looking

around at the photographs and paintings of dancers and opera singers and actors. Everyone was talking, but Tash had gone quiet. She'd been here a few times before with Mum, but she'd never walked across this floor surrounded by people her own age who loved ballet just as much as she did. She hoped that the other people in the audience could tell that they were ballet students. Coming here as an Aurora House student made her feel quite important!

Miss Anderbel led them to their seats, towards the back of the theatre but right in the middle, so they'd be able to see the whole stage even though they were quite far away. Tash took her seat and gazed up at the chandelier that hung from the high ceiling. She grinned when she noticed Dani and Anisha doing the same on either side of her. Then they all sat up properly again and peered at the rest of the audience.

"Look at that lady's outfit!" gasped Dani, pointing to the expensive seats below, where a woman was wearing a dress that looked like a ballgown.

"Wow," said Anisha. "I wonder if anyone will ever get dressed up like that to watch us dance."

"Ooh, look," said Tash, catching at Dani's arm. "That's Ms Hartley!"

They all followed Tash's pointing finger and saw the founder of their school dressed in a stylish skirt and jacket taking her seat in the front row.

The seats were almost all full now and the lights started to dim. Tash sat back and looked down at the stage, hidden by a blue velvet curtain the same colour as their school leotards. That colour – City Ballet Blue – linked Tash and her friends to the theatre and the dancers they were about to see, and she'd never felt so much a part of the ballet world as she did right then.

The Sleeping Beauty was perfect. It was everything that Tash had dreamed of when she'd thought about going to ballet school – from the cosy darkness of the theatre with her best friends on either side of her to the bright costumes onstage and the beautiful music rising from the orchestra and flowing around her – this was the world she wanted to live in. The dancers were brilliant and Tash was awed by their precise steps, which suited the music so exactly that it made her heart swell with joy.

She held her breath with her hands clasped to her chest during the famously difficult Rose Adagio, where the dancer playing Aurora had to balance on one leg *en pointe* with her other leg held up behind her in *attitude*. Four princes took turns to hold her hand and turn her round in a circle while she stayed balancing on one foot. Each time, when the circle was complete, the prince let go of her hand so that she was balancing all by herself for a moment before taking the hand of the next prince. She held the last balance for what seemed for ever before finishing it triumphantly – Tash finally started breathing again and the whole audience went wild with applause. She'd been so nervous, dreading that the dancer might fall, and now she felt thrilled. She made a silent promise to the theatre: one day she was going to make audiences feel like this too.

The next day, Tash woke up with the same determination and a little bit of horror. How could she have wasted a whole week? There might be no ballet classes during half-term, but there were still studios. All this time she could have been practising and she hadn't danced a single step. When there weren't so many people around it was harder to sneak off by herself, but she had to find a way. She was glad that she still had two more days before everyone else returned to school. She wasn't going to waste a minute of it.

"So Helen *finally* gave in," Dani announced at breakfast.

"About what?" Anisha asked through a mouthful of toast.

"Shopping, of course!" said Dani. "She'll take us today if we want."

"Duh," said Anisha. "We definitely want."

They both looked at Tash for her agreement.

"Um," Tash mumbled, scrambling for an excuse. "I can't…I forgot…I have homework."

"No you don't," said Dani. "We did all of it on Monday."

"Yeah, but…um…Mr Kent asked me to redo part of the English thing from last week."

Tash knew that she was going red with double guilt for breaking the school rules and telling an actual lie to her friends.

"That sucks," said Anisha. "I wish you could come with us."

"Me too," said Tash. "But I really need to get this done."

As soon as Dani, Anisha and Toril headed off with Helen and her friends, Tash grabbed her dance clothes and ran down to the door leading outside to the studios. She checked to make sure that no one had seen her slip out, then she hurried down the path and into the small studio building.

Tash knew that she had a lot of time to make up for. She'd seen so many amazing *pirouettes* in the City Ballet performance and she wanted to be just as good. What if having a week off dancing had made her lose the skills she'd worked so hard on for so many weeks? What if she couldn't do *pirouettes* properly any more in her first class back after the break? The thought of being criticized by Miss Anderbel again after the praise her teacher had given her on the coach to the theatre was awful. She *couldn't* let Miss Anderbel see that she'd slipped back. As long as her teachers thought she was improving, they wouldn't take her scholarship away.

At first her muscles felt stiff, so she did a proper warm-up at the *barre* and then went through all of the exercises they'd done in their last ballet class with Miss Anderbel – a slow, lovely *adage* with lots of balances and *developpés*, then *pirouettes*, small jumps and big leaps. Once she'd finished that, she went back to work on turns and then on jumps. Finally, with *The Sleeping Beauty* still firmly in her mind, she tried some of the steps she remembered from the Rose Adagio. She used the *barre* as her prince and practised standing in *attitude* on *demi-pointe* with one arm curved above her head. She let go of the *barre* and raised her other arm to fifth, seeing how long she could balance. It wasn't too difficult – long, slow balances had always been Tash's strength – but she knew it would be far, far harder in the pointe shoes that professional ballerinas wore.

Trying out steps from a real ballet felt wonderful and she couldn't wait until she was good enough to do them properly, *en pointe* and on a stage. Not only had her secret practice session soothed her fears, but she could see her life as a dancer stretching out in front of her. And she knew that she would do anything to make that happen.

Chapter 7

After half-term, the Year Seven girls and boys had all their afternoon dance classes together, and instead of contemporary and character dance, it was all ballet all the time. As Dani had guessed, they were starting to rehearse their performance for the Christmas fair.

They began their first afternoon rehearsal with a shortened version of their usual warm-up at the *barre* and then did some jumps in the centre of the room to make sure their muscles were ready to work hard.

"Great jumps, Tash," said Miss Anderbel, who was in charge of the Year Seven rehearsals. "I'd never guess you'd just had a week off. I don't think I've ever seen you get so high!"

Tash grinned. This was proof that her secret practice sessions were working! She still felt bad that she was breaking the rules, but it was having such a good effect on her dancing that she couldn't help also thinking that using the studio by herself was a brilliant idea.

"Everyone sit down for a moment," said Miss Anderbel, when they'd all caught their breath after the quick and energetic jumps. "I'm going to tell you about the piece we'll be dancing for the Christmas fair. The fair will be on a Saturday, the day after the end of term, so your performance there will be the last steps you dance before going home for the holidays. And as it's Christmas I don't think you'll be *very* surprised to hear you'll be dancing to music from *The Nutcracker*."

"Yesssss!" Tash heard all around her. She was pleased, too. Mum had taken her to see *The Nutcracker* a few times as a Christmas treat and the music always gave her a warm, festive glow inside.

"Quiet, please," Miss Anderbel said with a smile. "I want all of you to close your eyes and just listen. Pay attention to how the music makes you feel."

She started the music and Tash instantly recognized the children's dance at the party in Act One. A few people giggled at first, just because they were all sitting with their eyes closed, but within seconds everyone was silent as they drank in the cheerful, bright melody.

Keeping her eyes shut, Tash saw a giant sparkling Christmas tree, and a window with gently falling snow shimmering in the lights from the tree. She felt the frenzy of family and friends rushing all around her, the warmth of gingerbread and the unique taste of gold chocolate coins first thing in the morning. As the music wrapped around her, the Christmas from the stage and her own Christmases with Mum mixed together in her mind so that she was still Tash Marks, but also Clara in *The Nutcracker*, dancing with the special wooden doll, about to be whisked off to the Kingdom of Sweets.

"How did that make you feel?" Miss Anderbel asked when it finished.

"Like Christmas!" called Laura, and a lot of people agreed.

"Good start," said the teacher. "What else?"

"It feels exciting," said Toril. "Like something great is happening."

"It makes me want to get up and dance!" said Jonah.

He danced his feet on the floor where he sat and everyone laughed.

Miss Anderbel took a long time to pair each girl with a boy. These would be their partners for the rest of the term and she made sure they were height-matched so that they'd look good dancing together. Tash's partner was Rob, who often danced with Lily-May in *pas de deux* class, while Anisha was put with Nick. Dani, as everyone had guessed, was dancing with Jonah.

"What will our costumes be like?" asked Anisha, before they'd even got started on the dance.

"Oh, goodness, Anisha, I don't know!" exclaimed Miss Anderbel. "Let's learn at least a few steps first, shall we?"

"Okay," said Anisha, with a cheeky smile, and the class laughed.

They were in high spirits – the Christmassy music and the thrill of working towards a performance had got to all of them, and there was a buzz of excitement in everything they did. Miss Anderbel placed them in their pairs around the room and told them to hold hands with their arms crossed over each other so that they were both still facing the front. This caused a bit of confusion and a lot of giggling, and the teacher had to go around almost the whole class sorting them out.

"And I thought that was going to be the easy part," laughed Miss Anderbel. "You lot are meant to be the ballet dancers of the future!"

She taught them the beginning of the dance – they were going to be doing the traditional choreography used by City Ballet, which was intended for dancers their age. In the City Ballet performances, the children's roles were usually given to students in Year Eight at Aurora House – the Year Eights who'd been chosen this year had been showing off about it for weeks. They would be performing a couple of times a week during December with City Ballet, while the remaining half of Year Eight – those who were too tall to play little children or who simply hadn't danced well enough in the audition – would be rehearsing and performing another dance at the Christmas fair like the rest of the school.

Tash loved the skipping steps of the dance; they felt just right for excited children at a party. It was all quite easy so far and while Tash was dancing, she truly felt the Christmas joy that filled every note of the music. Her excitement was made even greater by the thought of performing to an audience as an Aurora House student for the first time. She imagined herself dancing with her friends in front of all their parents and teachers, and a thrill rushed through her whole body. It was going to be so much fun!

Preparations for the Christmas fair were suddenly the only thing anyone talked about.

"What are you guys doing?" Tash asked one of the Year Nines at their table that dinner time.

"Mr Edwards is choreographing something about ice skating for us," the girl replied importantly. "It's *so* cool having a dance created just for us!"

"We're doing *The Nutcracker*," said Anisha.

"So are Year Ten," said the girl. "Snowflakes. Well, the girls anyway. The boys must be doing something else. There's always loads of *The Nutcracker* at the Christmas fair."

"I love it," said Tash. "It's so...*Christmassy*!"

"Sixth Form are doing something super-classical that Mr Watkins is making up," said Dani, putting her tray down on the table next to Anisha. "And Year Eleven are contemporary."

"Any idea on Year Eight?" asked Tash. "The ones who aren't doing City Ballet, I mean."

"Nope," said Dani, "but I bet we'll hear as soon as we go into the common room."

As eager as Tash was to hear what Year Eight would be dancing at the Christmas fair, she had something more important to do after dinner.

"Hi, Tash," Mum said, answering the phone on the first ring. "Everything okay?"

"Will you come to the Christmas fair?" Tash blurted out. "It's on the last day of term so I know you're coming to pick me up. But please come early enough to see the fair as well! I'm dancing."

"Of course!" said Mum. "I'll put it in my diary right now."

Tash breathed a sigh of relief. By that time she'd have been at ballet school for a whole term and she'd have learned so much, especially if she kept up all her extra practice. And Mum would finally come, and the most important person in Tash's life would see her dance with the rest of Aurora House Ballet School.

Chapter 8

Tash couldn't help going back to the studios for a secret practice session that evening. If Mum was coming to see her dance, she wanted to be *perfect*. That meant making sure she got everything exactly right from the very beginning of rehearsals. Miss Anderbel had only taught them a short bit of the dance so far, but Tash wanted to go over it again and make sure she was doing it right. She couldn't allow herself to forget anything before the second rehearsal the next afternoon.

She flicked the lights on as she walked into the studio and dumped her bag in its usual place in the corner. She felt quite at home here by herself now. The first time it had been almost eerily quiet, but now she was comfortable with the silence, broken only by the soft sound of her ballet shoes padding and swishing across the floor.

She went through *barre* exercises and some centre practice, and then got on with the *Nutcracker* dance. She had the music on her iPod so she put her earphones in and put her iPod in her pocket, and went through the steps over and over again, making them certain and sure in her mind. Tash wanted the movement of her body to match the notes of the music so completely that she'd be able to do it without even thinking.

After working on the dance for ages, she was really tired, but she forced herself to keep going. She wanted to get in a bit of work on her *pirouettes* too. She'd just taken her earphones out when she heard a voice in the corridor outside. It was a teacher.

"Oh, hi, Natalia. Just checking who's using the studios! Carry on."

Tash felt sick. Natalia Garcia was in Year Eleven so she was allowed to use the studios by herself, but Tash wasn't. If the teacher, whoever it was, was checking in the studios, then she'd be opening all the doors, and Tash's studio was next. She had to think quickly. Her hand reached automatically for the light switch but then she realized that if the teacher saw the light go off, she'd know someone was hiding. Tash grabbed her bag and dived down behind the piano, her trailing iPod earphones flying out behind her and clacking on the top of the piano before landing across Tash's shoulders – just as the door opened.

"Anyone here?" the teacher asked.

It was Mrs O'Connell, who taught mostly the senior years. Tash held her breath and tried not to move. But she was crouching in an uncomfortable position and her ankles were wobbling.

"Leaving the lights on," Mrs O'Connell murmured. "So lazy."

She turned the lights off and walked out. Tash breathed out and allowed herself to slump down to the floor, her legs sticking out in front of her underneath the piano stool. That had been close.

The empty studio was suddenly the last place she wanted to be, so she gathered her things and ran guiltily back to the main building, checking over her shoulder constantly to make sure that nobody saw her.

For the next two weeks, morning ballet classes carried on as normal and Miss Anderbel taught them the dance for the Christmas fair in the afternoons. After almost getting caught, Tash was nervous about going back to the studios by herself. She wanted to carry on practising, but she really, really didn't want to get caught. So she just tried to work extra hard in ballet classes and to focus more than ever in rehearsals.

When she'd been in shows at her old dance school, she'd always got a bit sick of hearing the same music after rehearsing for weeks, but something about learning a dance for a performance at Aurora House was different. Tash felt the same excitement hearing the sparkling *Nutcracker* music every time she danced to it.

Then Miss Anderbel added a *pirouette* to the dance.

"There are a few counts while you girls are standing in place waiting for the boys to reach you," she said. "It would be good to fill those counts, and a *pirouette* would work nicely there. Can we go from the two circles, boys in a circle in the middle, girls in a circle around them...and skip out, two, three, four...then prepare, and two and *pirouette* – yes, that's it, Anisha!"

Tash *had* been getting better at *pirouettes* but she hadn't been able to practise them on her own for the last couple of weeks – so now she was worried. She was going to perform this dance in front of Mum, in front of the entire school, in front of all her teachers and all the other parents. It would be her first chance to show them how much she'd learned in her first term at Aurora House. The embarrassment she'd felt when she'd arrived late on the first day of term would be *nothing* compared to the shame she knew she'd feel if she messed the *Nutcracker* dance up in front of everyone who mattered to her.

In Friday morning's technique class, Miss Anderbel wanted to go over a section of the dance with the girls, and so they didn't have time to do all of the usual centre exercises. *Pirouettes* was one of the exercises their teacher skipped, and as the class went on, Tash got more and more anxious. Last time she'd done a *pirouette* she was sure she hadn't held her core well enough. She needed to practise!

After class, she hung back behind her friends as they all rushed out to the changing room. She knew that she didn't really have many seconds to waste – there was no way she'd have time to do a whole *pirouettes* exercise *and* get changed *and* make it to maths on time. Part of her felt that maths could wait, that learning about angles wasn't nearly as important as mastering the perfect double turn. But she knew that her maths teacher would have other ideas. Being on time for lessons and ballet classes and meals was one of the things the school was really strict about. It was supposed to teach them to be organized, because that would be useful in a dancer's career. But not as useful as a strong and precise double *pirouette*, Tash thought.

She faced the mirror and had a quick go at a double, but she only got one-and-a-half turns in before she fell off *demi-pointe*. She took a deep breath and focused, ready to try again. Next time she managed two turns, but it wasn't as neat as she wanted. She frowned at herself in the mirror. Then she noticed Lily-May further back in the studio, preparing to do a *pirouette* herself. Tash suddenly felt hopeful. Maybe she wasn't the only one who was worried about performing *pirouettes* in the dance!

"I love the dance for the fair, but I wish we had more time to work on technique," said Lily-May a few minutes later, as they both walked out to the changing room. "An hour a day just isn't enough."

"Uh…yeah," Tash agreed, surprised. They hadn't spoken much since the first day of term in Mr Kent's class. "I'm worried I'm going to mess up the *pirouettes* in the dance."

"Because you'll be so nervous? Lots of people are at first, you know. It's so important to keep practising, isn't it?"

"Are you worried about that too?" Tash asked.

"Oh, I don't get nervous," Lily-May replied easily. She smiled at Tash and then went to the opposite side of the changing room where she'd left her things.

Tash stared after her for a moment. She hadn't even *thought* about the fact that feeling nervous in the performance might make it even harder to dance well. Lily-May knew loads about ballet training because her parents had both been dancers. If she thought they should be doing extra practice, then she was probably right. She was the best dancer in their year and if Tash wanted to be just as good, then she should take Lily-May's advice.

It was time to start the secret practice sessions again. She had to make sure that even nerves wouldn't throw her *pirouettes* off balance on the day of the performance. And the only way to do that was to practise, practise, practise.

Later that evening, Tash decided to sneak across to the studios to do some more work.

"Where are you going?" asked Anisha, seeing Tash pick up her bag.

"I'm calling my mum," Tash replied. "It's so

noisy in the common room, and Toril and Laura are up in the dorm. I thought I'd go and sit in our form room."

"Oh, good idea!" said Anisha. "See you later."

Tash pretended to head towards their form room, and then ducked into the corridor that led outside. She hurried down the path to the studio block, trying not to think about how horrible it felt to lie to her friend. She wished she didn't have to, but she couldn't see any other way; it was so important that no one found out how much extra practice she needed. Besides, if she owned up to it now, they'd know that she'd lied to them before.

She tiptoed down the corridor between the studios, peeking in through the windows to check for teachers. It didn't look as if there were any around. Tash found a small studio that was empty and put her things down in one corner. Then she changed rapidly into dance clothes and got to work.

Even though it always felt much better to

dance to music, Tash was scared that if she had her earphones in, she might not be able to hear a teacher coming. So she danced in silence.

After weeks of *barre* exercises followed by repeating the joyful steps of the *Nutcracker* dance over and over again, it felt good to push her muscles more than she did in rehearsals. She ran through the exercises they usually did in class, going through everything twice and watching every movement in the mirror, checking for places where her shape wasn't quite right or where she needed to turn out more. It took much longer than a usual class because she repeated everything until the movements were as good as she could possibly get them. After that, she was tired, but she went back to *pirouettes* and jumps again anyway because they were the two areas where she really thought she needed to improve.

By the end, she was exhausted, and she didn't feel that good. The extra practice didn't seem to be helping as much as before. In fact, it seemed as if the harder she pushed herself, the messier her turns became, and the lower her jumps were. She wanted ballet to make her feel good again.

"That's what all this work is for," she said aloud in the silent studio. "If you work hard and get perfect, then it will *feel* perfect."

But there was a quick fix, too. She knew that the *Nutcracker* dance was just the dance of joy that she needed to feel better. She dug around in her bag for her iPod, plugged in one earphone, leaving one ear able to hear if a teacher was coming, selected the music and tucked the small device into her pocket. As the *Nutcracker* music started, she began to dance, a smile spreading further across her face with every step.

"Great jumps, Tash!" Miss Anderbel called the next week while they were halfway through the dance.

Tash glowed with pride. It was working! The extra practice *was* helping her get better! Now all she had to do was keep at it, however exhausted it made her feel.

"Okay, we're going to take a break," said Miss Anderbel, when they'd finished running through the dance. "And I think you're all going to enjoy it."

Tash looked at Dani, who shrugged to say she had no idea either.

"Costumes!" cried their teacher. "Exciting, right?" Everyone started to talk at once, wondering what the costumes would be. "We've had these ones for a few years, so I need you all to try them on and we can see if we have to make any adjustments."

The teacher went out of the studio and came back pulling a rack of clothes – beautiful dresses with ribbons and lace in loads of different colours for the girls, and frilly shirts and trousers for the boys. They all sat down on the floor and drank from their bottles of water while Miss Anderbel looked through the costumes and handed them out according to height and size. When it was her turn to go up, Tash took the soft material of the dress in her hands and gazed at the pale-blue ribbons with delight. It was so pretty!

They all hurried off to the changing rooms and for a while the only sounds were gasps of happiness as the girls pulled on the dresses and tied the ribbons around their waists. The soft material hung in folds below their knees, and the top layer on Tash's white dress shimmered slightly in the bright lights of the changing room. Dani was in cream and red, which suited her blonde hair and rosy cheeks, while Anisha's dress was trimmed with dark green. They all twirled around, letting their skirts fly out around them, looking down at themselves in wonder.

"Picture time!" said Dani, grabbing her phone from her bag.

She snapped a photo of the three of them standing together, smiling. Then they all crowded their heads together to see it.

"We look so pretty!" Tash said in surprise, and they smiled widely at each other for a moment before heading back to the studio, where the boys were comparing their costumes, pretending not to be embarrassed by all the frills on their shirts.

"You look really pretty," Rob said to Tash, when they were standing in place, ready for their very first dress rehearsal.

Tash blushed a bit and giggled. "So do you."

Miss Anderbel asked them to go through the dance without the music once so that they could get used to the costumes and find out if there were any places where the dresses got in the way of the steps. Then they ran it with the music. The third time, Miss Anderbel got out a video camera.

"I want to film it so I can see the whole thing at once," she explained. "And then I can really check to see which bits we need to work on."

Tash suddenly felt nervous. Once, at her old dance school, someone had made a video of one of their shows, but that had been on a dark stage and the camera had been far away. It would be impossible to ignore Miss Anderbel filming right here.

But as soon as the music started and she began to dance and whirl around the room, surrounded by friends in pretty dresses, she *did* forget about it. She forgot about the studio and the mirrors, too, and the late-night practice session she had ahead of her. She was just a girl in a lovely dress, dancing at a party.

Chapter 9

"There you are!" said Dani, as Tash came back into the main building after yet another hard-working solo session in the small studio. "It's your turn to pick the film tonight. Where have you been?"

"Oh…I forgot. I was talking to my mum." Tash hid her ballet shoes and dance clothes behind her back as she spoke.

"I thought you said she was really busy this

week and you wouldn't get to speak to her? Is everything okay?"

"Um, she is. She was calling to tell me about her work trip. I'm just...I need to get something from the dorm, I'll see you in the common room."

Upstairs, Tash stuffed her dance clothes into the pile of things that needed to be washed and put her ballet shoes back in their drawer. Then she ran back down to the common room, where she flopped, exhausted, onto the sofa next to Anisha.

"What are we watching, Tash?" asked Rob, kneeling by the DVD shelves.

"I don't mind," sighed Tash.

She was way too tired to think about which film she wanted to see.

"Noooo!" wailed Dani. "You *have* to pick or Jonah will make us watch *Mary Poppins*. AGAIN."

"It's got good dancing!" protested Jonah.

"Yeah, and the songs get stuck in everyone's head for a week afterwards," retorted Dani.

Tash laughed. "It's nearly Christmas. What

about *The Nutcracker*? I know there's a City Ballet DVD somewhere."

"No!" shouted almost everyone, and Anisha hit Tash with a cushion.

Tash couldn't help laughing.

"Okay, okay! *Home Alone*?" she suggested, as it caught her eye on the shelf. That was a Christmas classic, and it was fun. No concentrating required, just what was needed.

She settled into the film with her friends, thinking about how it was totally impossible to get left home alone by mistake when you lived at a boarding school. It was nice. Dani and Laura had both squashed onto the sofa, too, so they were all tightly packed together. Tash felt very cosy, and so tired. Less than twenty minutes into the film, she fell asleep, her head dropping down onto Anisha's shoulder.

"I think I'm too tired for this rehearsal," Tash admitted to her friends on the way to the studio one Tuesday morning in the first week of December.

The performance was only two weeks away, and she'd spent even longer than usual dancing by herself the night before. She was exhausted. She held her arm out to open the door to the studio block and almost stumbled straight into it with the effort of trying to push it open.

"Uh-oh," giggled Anisha. "We've still got four days of rehearsals until the weekend."

"Are you okay, Tash?" Dani asked as they trooped into the changing room and Tash immediately sat on the bench, dropping her bag on the floor.

"Yeah," Tash said with a sigh. "Just tired. All the rehearsals. You know."

"That's all? You sure? You seem…" began Dani.

"…kind of distant," finished Anisha. "And you're *always* tired."

"Is it…home…or anything?" Dani asked in an awkwardly halting voice.

"It's nothing," said Tash. "I'm fine."

Professional dancers spent all day long in rehearsals, and then they performed in the evenings. Admitting that she was tired from too much dancing would show everyone that she wasn't cut out to be a professional ballerina after all.

"Okay…" said Dani, but Tash saw the look that passed between her and Anisha. They were worried about her.

They were using that morning's ballet class for a rehearsal again, and Tash made mistake after mistake. When Miss Anderbel asked them to go left she went right, and she got her feet muddled up, nearly tripping over Rob three times. Miss Anderbel kept shooting her worried looks, but she didn't say anything, which made Tash even more anxious. She knew she was dancing badly. Why wasn't her teacher correcting her? Was it because she was so bad that she wasn't even worth correcting?

After she'd got the timing completely wrong in the jumps for the second time, Tash felt like storming out of the studio and not coming back. Dani and Anisha came to comfort her when they took a break.

"Bad day," grimaced Dani. "I had one last week, remember?"

Tash did remember, and it made her feel a bit better. In a rehearsal the week before, Dani had managed to forget almost every step of the *Nutcracker* dance. She had driven the whole class mad by messing it up so much that they all had to start again from the beginning at least six times in five minutes.

"You'll do better this afternoon," offered Anisha. "Or tomorrow."

Tash nodded. She was going to make sure that she did. This evening, she'd work on the dance until there was no chance she'd ever mess it up again.

Chapter 10

The *Nutcracker* dance no longer felt like a lovely way to feel the joy of really and truly dancing. That evening, it was serious. She was going to make sure that she could do it perfectly. The Christmas fair would be the first time Mum saw Tash perform with Aurora House Ballet School, and it was also her chance to show her teachers that she was good enough to be there. It was what the whole term's hard work had been leading up to.

Ballet Stars

After dinner, Tash told her friends she was going to Skype with Mum and dragged her exhausted feet down the path to the studios. She started her usual warm-up at the *barre* but her muscles soon felt warm and she was eager to get to the dance. She skipped some of the exercises that focused on small, quick movements of the feet and moved straight on to *grands battements*.

When Tash finished her quick warm-up, she put on the *Nutcracker* music and got to work. She went through the dance five times in a row without making a single mistake, and couldn't help smiling when she caught sight of herself flying round the room in the mirror. It felt amazing, and she wished that she had been able to dance this well in the rehearsals earlier. She stared at her reflection while holding her finishing pose, and focused her energy into a determination to dance like this at the Christmas fair.

Tash paused to take a drink of water but wouldn't let herself sit down, afraid that if she did, she wouldn't get back up again. She'd promised herself she'd work on jumps, and she wasn't leaving until they were as good as Lily-May's.

She faced the mirror and performed the jumps sequence that she'd messed up in the morning rehearsal. She could get the timing perfectly now, and her jumps were neat and pretty. But they weren't high enough. The second time, she flew higher into the air but she lost a little of the neatness, and to Tash, that was not acceptable. She knew it wouldn't be good enough for City Ballet either. She had to try again, but she was exhausted.

She drank from her water bottle until there was none left. She didn't think she had enough energy left in her for another round of *entrechats*. But as soon as that thought entered her head, she threw the bottle down.

"You're not finished yet, Natasha Marks," she told her reflection. "You're not done until you're perfect."

She prepared in fifth and jumped up into an

entrechat quatre, crossing her feet over and back again in the air so that she landed with the same foot in front. She did another one, pushing herself up into the air as high as she could.

But this time she landed hard on her right foot, her ankle twisting under her weight. She cried out in pain and fell forwards onto her hands and knees, then sat back holding her foot and gritting her teeth. She choked away the tears that were already falling, took a deep breath and tried to stand. She knew immediately that she couldn't – her ankle hurt way too much and she was terrified of making it worse.

Tash's hands were shaking and a tumbled mix of pain and fear filled her head. What if she'd seriously injured herself? What if she'd never be able to dance again? She tried desperately to shut out all the other *what ifs* crowding into her brain and held on to her hurt ankle with both hands.

She was starting to get cold, and she knew that was bad for her other muscles. Somehow she had to get back to the dorm, but she couldn't walk by herself, and no one knew she was here. She sniffed and wiped her face – wet from tears and sweat – with the back of her hand. She could figure this out. Her hoody wasn't too far away: ten steps, maybe fifteen. If she could only get to it, she'd at least be warm, and she'd work the rest out from there.

Tash put her hands down on the floor, ready to push herself up and try to stand. Then the door crashed open and Dani and Anisha stood there, staring at her.

They rushed to her side, Anisha almost sliding across the floor as she tried to get down next to Tash as quickly as possible.

"What happened?" demanded Dani.

"Are you hurt?" asked Anisha at the same time.

"My ankle," Tash whispered.

Tash saw Dani's eyes dart around the room. Within seconds, she had shot away and back again and was pulling Tash's hoody over her head, helping her put her arms through the sleeves.

"Thanks," Tash said, hugging the warm navy-blue Aurora House hoody close to her. "How did you know I was here?"

"We saw you take your ballet shoes out of the dorm earlier, and when you didn't come back for ages and ages we decided to come and find you," said Anisha. "We got worried."

"What did you do?" Dani asked again.

"I was – practising," said Tash, her voice breaking in her effort not to cry again. "*Entrechats*. I think – I landed – wrong…"

"How bad?" asked Anisha. "Do you think it's broken?"

"I don't know!" cried Tash, and she looked up at her friends in terror. What if it *was* broken? What if it could never be properly healed? Had she just ended her dance career aged eleven? "It can't be! I need to dance."

She broke down completely then and, as her tired body shook with sobs, Dani and Anisha shuffled closer on the floor and hugged her until she'd calmed down.

"We need to tell someone," Anisha said gently. "You should see Dr Stevens."

Tash nodded miserably. That was the sensible thing to do. But if she was going to find out that she'd never dance professionally, she wanted to put off hearing it for as long as possible.

"I'll go," said Dani.

She gave Tash a quick hug before she ran out of the studio to get help from the school doctor. Anisha leaned her head against Tash's and hugged her again while they waited.

"It's not broken," said Dr Stevens, and Tash was so relieved that she cried again.

"Thank goodness," murmured Miss Anderbel, standing anxiously above Tash.

Dani had run into their teacher on her way to get Dr Stevens and explained what had happened, and Miss Anderbel had hurried to the studio to help. Now they were sure the ankle wasn't broken, Miss Anderbel and the doctor helped Tash to stand and move into a chair.

"It's a nasty sprain, though," Dr Stevens continued. "You won't be able to dance for at least three weeks."

"But – the Christmas fair!" protested Tash. "That's next week!"

"I'm sorry," said Dr Stevens. "I can't allow it. Not unless you want to do further damage. Rest, calm and *no dancing* is what you need."

"But—" Tash began.

"If you don't follow my advice, you could end your dancing career over this."

Tash shut her mouth immediately. She'd give almost anything to dance with her friends at the Christmas fair. Almost. The one thing she *wouldn't* give up was her chance at a life dancing with City Ballet.

"Well, you're free to go," said the doctor, when

she'd finished strapping a support bandage around Tash's ankle.

"No you're not," said Miss Anderbel. "I want to talk to you."

Tash went red and looked down at her injured foot. Dr Stevens gathered her things and left. Dani and Anisha had already gone – they'd wanted to stick around to find out if Tash's ankle was broken, but Miss Anderbel had sent them back to the dormitory to get some warm clothes for Tash.

"What were you *thinking*?" demanded the teacher, and suddenly the thing that hurt the most wasn't Tash's ankle, but the knowledge that Miss Anderbel was disappointed in her.

"I wanted to be perfect," Tash replied honestly, meeting her teacher's eyes.

Miss Anderbel sighed. "Tash, when people say 'practice makes perfect', they don't mean you should do all the practice in one go. What makes a dancer great isn't pushing technique until you can't push any more, it's time. Time, experience, *years* of hard work. That's why we train students for seven years before we send them out to dance with ballet companies, and it's why we don't allow our younger students to practise alone."

"But I was getting there," said Tash. "My *pirouettes* and jumps got better."

"Yes," agreed Miss Anderbel. "And then they got worse. I know that you're passionate and you want to be the best dancer you can be, and those are some of the things that will make you great one day. But tiring yourself out until dancing becomes a chore won't help."

Miss Anderbel looked seriously at Tash, and Tash nodded, finally understanding.

"In the audition we saw a girl who loved ballet for the way it made her feel," continued Miss Anderbel. "And in classes at the beginning of term, watching you enjoying every step gave me so much pleasure. That's the reason we wanted you at the school enough to offer you a full scholarship. I want that girl back in my classes, please. Because *that's* the Natasha Marks who's going to dance Odette in *Swan Lake* one day and she's going to make *so many* audiences fall in love with ballet."

"Do you really think so?" Tash whispered.

"I really do," replied Miss Anderbel. "That's what you want, isn't it?"

"More than anything," said Tash.

"Never forget that," said the teacher. "It's hard to make an audience feel the joy of ballet if you're not feeling it yourself. Brilliant technique will come to you in time, if you work hard in your classes. But if you push yourself so hard that you're not enjoying it any more, you'll lose the thing that makes you such a special dancer, and you'll get hurt. You're very lucky that this injury isn't worse. Believe me, you don't want to risk injuring yourself so badly that you have to give up your career."

Tash remembered that that was what had happened to Miss Anderbel and she nodded seriously.

"I'm sorry," she said.

Everything that Miss Anderbel said made so much sense. Tash wished she hadn't been so silly. Now she wouldn't get to dance at the Christmas fair and show Mum the joy of dancing that Miss Anderbel saw in her.

She deserved to be told off for being so stupid, but Miss Anderbel was being so nice to her; her friends should hate her for lying to them, but instead they had just tumbled through the door with her clothes and kept hugging her to make her feel better. Tash hugged them back and smiled at Miss Anderbel. Dani and Anisha helped her off the chair where she'd been sitting and she picked up the crutches that the doctor had given her to use until she was able to walk again.

Tash sighed, and swung herself forward on the crutches. She'd always thought crutches looked kind of fun, but as she gripped them and thought about trying to get up the stairs to Coppélia, she realized that had been an idiotic thing to think. She'd been an idiot about so many things. All that stupid extra practice and now she was stuck on stupid crutches and she'd have to do stupid sitting down calmly instead of ballet classes, and, worst of all, stupid watching instead of dancing at the Christmas fair. And the worst thing was that it was all her own fault.

"Hi, Mum," she said in a shaky voice as soon as Mum answered the phone.

She knew she had to tell Mum what had happened, but she felt sick at the thought of it. She was going to have to admit that she'd been breaking the school rules and Mum would be so disappointed in her.

"Hi!" Mum replied cheerfully. "How are rehearsals going? I'm so excited about watching you dance next week!"

Mum sounded so happy. Tash had no idea how to break her news.

"I can't dance at the fair!" she cried, the words rushing out of her before she'd worked out a better way to say it.

"Why? What's happened?" asked Mum, and Tash could hear the instant worry in her voice.

"I've...hurt my ankle," Tash managed to say before her voice went high-pitched and full of tears, and she cried down the phone because her ankle was painful and because she couldn't dance.

Nothing would ever hurt as much as this.

Chapter 11

Tash had had no idea how hard it would be to watch her classmates dancing without her. The next afternoon, Miss Anderbel said that she could sit on a chair in a corner of the studio during the rehearsal. Seeing the *Nutcracker* dance as part of the audience instead of being in the middle of it, Tash realized how good it was. Everyone had worked so hard to learn the steps and now it was all about performing it well the next week –

and Year Seven were definitely going to do that.

At first, Dani and Anisha kept smiling at her, but once they got stuck into the rehearsal, they seemed to forget about her. Everyone was completely focused on the steps and Miss Anderbel's corrections. Sarah from Year Eight had been asked to learn the dance quickly and take Tash's place; Tash could hardly look at her. Rob had been worried about Tash when she'd come into the common room on crutches, and then he'd been worried about dancing with a new partner, but now he and Sarah were completely absorbed in the rehearsal, dancing and laughing as if they'd been partners for ages. Tash tried to focus on the others instead, but even that was difficult. They were all off in ballet-land, and Tash was left outside by herself. It felt horrible. Dancing perfectly didn't seem to matter so much now; that afternoon, she would have been thrilled to be able to dance *at all*.

"Tash, Mr Watkins wants to talk to you in his office," said Chris, one of the Year Eight boys, poking his head around the studio door while the class were listening to Miss Anderbel's corrections.

Tash sent a startled look to Dani and Anisha, who gave her a mixture of anxious glances and thumbs up for luck from the other side of the room. Tash took a deep breath and grabbed her crutches. Mr Watkins was the headteacher, and she was dreading what he would say to her.

"I hope you understand how silly you've been," Mr Watkins began, when Tash was settled in a chair opposite his desk.

She nodded silently.

"Our classes and timetables are structured very carefully," he continued. "If you don't believe that our classes are enough, perhaps you shouldn't be at Aurora House."

Tash felt her stomach spinning around inside her. Did this mean…?

"Of course, that would be a great shame," Mr Watkins said, his face still stern. "I'd hate to lose one of the most promising dancers we have."

Tash smiled hesitantly and she felt the smile grow into a big grin as his words sunk in. Mr Watkins thought she was promising!

"Thank you," she managed to say.

"If I *ever* have to talk to you about this again, you won't find me giving out so many compliments," said Mr Watkins.

"You won't have to," replied Tash meekly. "I came to Aurora House because I love dancing. And now that I'm here, I want to learn everything I can and be the best dancer I can possibly be. But Miss Anderbel helped me understand that I mustn't forget to love what I'm doing. And not to push myself too hard."

"It's a difficult balance to learn," said Mr Watkins. "Your determination will help you succeed, but it can also ruin your chances if you use it the wrong way. Don't let that happen. You can go now."

Tash pulled herself to her feet.

"Trust us, Tash," Mr Watkins said with a smile, as she hobbled out of his office. "We do know what we're doing."

Mum phoned later to see how Tash was, and Tash told her everything that Mr Watkins had said.

"So, are you feeling better?" Mum asked.

"A bit," said Tash. "It's really horrible watching everyone rehearse without me. I wish I didn't have to see them all dance at the Christmas fair."

"Oh, darling, I know it must be hard," said Mum. "Do you want to come home? I have a meeting tomorrow but I can come up and get you afterwards. And I can cancel my work plans for next week."

"No, Mum, you don't need to do that..." Tash protested weakly, even though going home and getting a cuddle from Mum was suddenly exactly what she wanted.

"Tash, it's fine. If you want to come home now, I'll make it work."

"Maybe," said Tash. "I want to see you. But there's school…"

"Ask your teachers," suggested Mum. "And if they say it's okay, send me a text and I'll drive up as soon as my meeting's finished tomorrow morning."

"Thanks, Mum. I love you."

"I love you, my little dancer."

Tash bit her lip when Mum hung up the phone. She sat there in lovely, cosy Coppélia and stared around. Her bed was still piled with the stuffed toys the others had lent her to make her feel better, and she hugged Dani's soft cat to her chest along with Anisha's battered old teddy bear and her own faded pink bunny rabbit. She remembered the beginning of the term when she'd worried that she'd be the only one childish enough to bring an old stuffed animal with her, and the laughter when they'd all realized that everyone had brought something to comfort them in their first weeks away from home.

As always, Dani's bed was neatly made and Anisha's looked as if she'd tidied up her things while blindfolded. There were ballet shoes all over the place and leotards and school uniforms hanging on the front of wardrobes and draped over chairs. Brightly coloured magazines were splayed out across Laura's bed, and Toril's Norwegian–English dictionary had been dumped on hers next to a stack of school books, while Donna's little area looked as if it had been hit by a glitter-hurricane. The Christmas decorations they'd all made together a couple of days ago were strung up around the room, but it looked as if they'd got more glitter on Donna's bed than on the snowflakes and paper chains. It was school, but it felt like home.

Tash had never realized, until that moment, that home could be two places at once. It was the comfort of Mum, far away, but it was the fun of friends at school, too. It was feeling that you belonged.

"Guess what we're watching!" said Dani, bursting into the room with Anisha just behind her.

"What?" Tash asked, with a smile.

"*Guess*," insisted Dani.

"No, there's no time!" cried Anisha. "Come on!"

Tash followed them down to the common room as fast as she could on crutches. Lily-May got up from the chair she was on and offered it to Tash, and Anisha put down a cushion on the floor for her to rest her foot on.

"We know you've been wanting to watch it for ages," said Dani.

Laura pressed play on the remote control and the dark screen came to life. Familiar music started to play, and a blue velvet curtain rose on a stage filled with the stars and lights of Christmas. *The Nutcracker*. Anisha put her arm around Tash and gave her a hug. Tash leaned her head against Anisha's for a moment, and then settled into the chair as the music filled her from her ears to her toes.

Everyone got excited when the music for their dance came on and they watched the children in the City Ballet performance do the steps they would be doing at the Christmas fair. Tash tried to be excited along with them. It still hurt that she wouldn't get to perform, but her friends seemed to know exactly how she was feeling, because Dani leaned over and gave her arm a quick squeeze and Anisha bent her head close to whisper, "Next year we'll do something even better than this."

As they watched the cast bowing for the audience at the end of the performance, Tash pulled out her phone and sent a text to Mum: *I want to stay here until the end of term. Don't need to come home early. See you at the Christmas fair, I can't wait for you to meet everyone! xx*

Chapter 12

After their last rehearsal on the final day of lessons, Tash and her friends were so excited that none of them could sit down for long. They ate dinner quickly and then hurried back up to Coppélia to pack everything they wanted to take home for the Christmas holidays.

"Tash, is your homework diary in the common room with mine?" asked Dani. "I'm going down now, if you've left anything there."

"Yeah, I guess I *should* take my homework diary with me. And that book I borrowed from Lucy. I think I left it on the shelf. Will you see if it's there? Anisha, is this your pencil case?"

"*There* it is!" cried Anisha, as Dani left the room. "Oh, has Dani gone? I wanted to borrow some of her *Friends* DVDs." And she ran out of the room after Dani.

At last everything was packed and six suitcases sat at the ends of beds, waiting to be carried off home by parents the next afternoon. The girls sat up in bed after lights-out, talking about their plans for the three weeks off.

"I'm going to go ice skating next week," said Donna.

"Don't break any bones!" said Tash with a look of horror. She didn't need the crutches any more but her foot still hurt if she tried to jump or do anything more than walk.

"I'll try," laughed Donna.

"I'm going to *not dance*," said Anisha.

"Yeah, right," said Laura. "I bet none of us can go three weeks without it."

"I'll have to," said Tash. But she tried to stay cheerful. "My foot should be better by the last week of the holidays, though. So I'll start practising again as soon as I'm allowed!"

Everyone woke up really early next morning. They were all so excited about dancing for their parents at the Christmas fair, having fun with their friends, and going home for the holidays afterwards. Tash wriggled down further under the duvet and pretended to be asleep for a little while longer. She couldn't wait to see Mum, but she still felt envious that her friends would all get to dance their piece from *The Nutcracker* and she'd have to sit at the side and watch them doing the steps without her.

"Tash, are you awake?" she heard from the bed next to hers.

Tash rolled onto her other side to face Anisha

and mumbled a good morning.

"How are you feeling?" Anisha asked.

Tash grimaced.

"We're first on our class stall, remember," said Dani. "That'll be fun."

"Yeah, that'll help," agreed Tash.

Year Seven had asked each of the teachers for a photo of themselves as a child so people at the fair could have a go at guessing who was who. The person who got the most right would win a prize. They'd spent ages giggling at the photos in their classroom and had refused to let anyone else see them until the day of the fair, where they would be displayed on big boards decorated with paper snowflakes, glitter and drawings of characters from *The Nutcracker*. Tash remembered that she was actually really excited about watching the rest of the school trying to figure out who the children in the photos were. The photo of Mr Watkins as a baby was hilarious, and she bet that no one would guess it correctly – he was dressed in a christening gown and had big, pretty blue eyes. He really looked like a girl!

She got out of bed and dressed in a black dress with white flowers on it, and then pulled a pale grey jumper on over the top. The sky outside was a matching shade of light, icy grey. Tash wondered if it was going to snow and she shivered both with the cold and with the delight of Christmas. She brushed her long, dark hair and let it hang down her back. It felt strange to leave it down while the others were busily putting theirs up for their performance.

At last they were all ready, and they clattered downstairs, talking noisily and gasping in awe at the beautiful Christmas decorations that had gone up all over the school. The big Christmas tree had been in the dining hall for the last two weeks and most year groups had put tinsel and paper chains up in their classrooms, but overnight the corridors had been transformed into a sparkling Christmas wonderland. Brightly coloured tinsel and silvery fairy-lights framed the noticeboards, branches of holly lay along the tops of picture frames, and red and gold baubles hung from every possible place.

"It's like that bit in *The Nutcracker* when the Christmas tree magically grows taller and taller!" Tash said to Dani.

"Maybe the tree in the dining room will be three times bigger than it was yesterday!" joked Dani.

It wasn't, but they all gasped when they saw it anyway. The Christmas tree had been beautiful before, sprinkled with shiny silver threads and decorations shaped like ballerinas and angels and Nutcrackers and penguins with santa hats, but now it was even brighter, and shone with the vivid colours of candy canes and the gold wrappers of little chocolate bears, which had appeared overnight. Tash and her friends ran to the tree and stood exclaiming at everything new that caught their eyes. There was quite a crowd building up around it, and Miss Anderbel soon came over to get them moving.

"Parents will be arriving in an hour and a half," she reminded them. "Hurry up with breakfast, you've still got to get your class stalls ready."

The dancers did as they were told, and gulped down their usual breakfast of juice and cereal. Once they'd finished, they went to their form room to help get their stall ready. Year Seven only needed one table for people to use to write down their guesses, so Mr Kent told them to take one from the classroom and move it out into the main corridor. He produced some red crêpe paper for them to use as a tablecloth, and a tube of gold glitter. Rob, Nick, Lily-May and Laura stuck the photo boards to the wall behind their table while Tash, Anisha and Dani laid out the tablecloth. Dani took the lid off the glitter tube to scatter some onto the table, but she was too eager and it all rushed out in one big golden mess.

"Dani!" said Anisha and Tash at the same time, and everyone laughed.

"It's fine!" said Dani and she spread the glitter across the table with her hands. "See!"

She held up her hands, now completely covered in gold specks, and grinned widely at her friends.

"What?" she asked, seeing their expressions. "I'll bring the *sparkle* to our dance."

Tash and Anisha burst out laughing all over again. They were so excited about the Christmas holidays and the fair that everything seemed funnier, brighter and more wonderful than usual.

Parents began to arrive and students wandered around the fair in groups. The Year Seven stall was a popular attraction for everyone. Tash bit back a grin every time someone guessed that the photo of Mr Watkins was one of the female teachers.

"Is that Mrs Harris?" asked Chris from Year Eight.

"I couldn't possibly tell you," said Dani, all innocence.

"Oh, I just have *no* idea," added Anisha.

"Whatever," said Chris, rolling his eyes. "You know we can just sneak a look at the answers when you guys are dancing."

"You can't," retorted Dani. "Tash is going to be Guardian of the Answers."

Tash nodded, but her bright smile fell away as she remembered that she *wouldn't* be dancing. Anisha put an arm around her and she felt a little better. And then she suddenly felt a *lot* better – as she spotted a much-loved face heading her way.

"Mum!" she cried.

Mum pushed through the crowd by the Year Eight stall next to Tash's table, and Tash fumbled past her friends and ran into Mum's arms.

"How's your ankle?" Mum asked, as soon as

she'd finished hugging Tash and kissing the top of her head.

"It's okay," said Tash. "But I still can't dance. I really wanted you to see me."

Mum made a sympathetic face. "I know, and I wish that I could, but I'm just happy to be here with you! I've missed you so much."

"I've missed you, too," said Tash and pulled Mum towards her for another hug.

"So, what's going on here?" Mum asked, when Tash let her go. Tash grinned and pulled Mum over to the Year Seven stall.

"Mum, this is Dani and Anisha. They're my best friends ever, ever."

"Hi," said Dani and Anisha in unison. Then Dani looked at her watch and grabbed at Anisha's arm. "We've got to go!" she said. "We're dancing in ten minutes and we're still not changed!"

"Go! Go!" said Tash. "Oh, wait!"

They turned back and Tash pulled them both in for a group hug.

"Good luck," she told them, and she really meant it. If Mum couldn't see what *she* could do, she wanted her to see her best friends dance well instead. "We should go and find seats for the performance," she said to Mum.

She folded up the answer sheet for the stall and slipped it into her small shoulder bag. She didn't think anyone really would cheat, but she wanted to make sure. Her class were relying on her.

Tash and Mum managed to get seats in the front row. The school had a small theatre with tiered seating, but there were so many parents and friends here to watch that there weren't enough seats for everyone. Loads of people were standing down the sides of the room and at the back, too. There was a big projector screen set up at the back of the stage. Tash wondered briefly what it was for, but guessed it was probably for the Year Eleven contemporary piece.

"The first group is our Year Seven girls and

boys," announced Miss Anderbel, when the large audience of parents was ready. "They've all worked incredibly hard on this dance from *The Nutcracker*, but unfortunately one of the dancers who worked the hardest is unable to perform today. Natasha Marks is injured and she's having to miss out." Tash felt herself turning red. "But we couldn't let her dancing go completely unseen, so in an Aurora House Christmas Fair first, we're going to see live dancing and a video recording at the same time."

A murmur went around the room and Tash sat up straight in her chair with wide eyes. What video? What was Miss Anderbel talking about? The screen flickered to life and she saw the big studio they'd used for the dress rehearsal. Of course! Miss Anderbel had filmed the dance! She tried to remember how well she'd danced that day, but the rehearsals had all blurred together because she'd been so tired from all her extra practice.

"Well, I think we're ready," said Miss Anderbel, "so I'm going to hand over to Year Seven to get you all in a festive mood."

Tash was about to find out exactly how well she'd danced. And so was everyone else.

Tash's class ran onto the stage and took up their places. The music started and as the dancers onstage began to move, the video on the screen started playing too, so perfectly in time with the music that it was like looking through a big window into a studio behind the stage. Tash watched herself dancing on screen, skipping and spinning around the bright studio with her lovely white and blue dress flying out around her and she felt so happy, because it was almost as if she wasn't missing out at all. She would have loved to be dancing up there with her friends, but this was the next best thing. And it meant she got to watch her friends too.

Her eyes followed Dani and Anisha around the stage – they were both really good! They were so different from each other, too. In fact, everyone in the class was brilliant in a totally unique way. Lily-May had the elegance and grace of a princess and everything she did was precise, while Anisha performed the same movements with so much expression that you felt like she really was the character she was pretending to be, and Dani danced dreamily, bringing fairy-lightness to the quick, pretty steps.

Tash watched herself dancing on the screen in time with her friends in the room, and suddenly she understood what she hadn't been able to see before. There were things that she was the best at and there were things that she wasn't so good at, but it wasn't any of those individual elements that defined who she was as a dancer. It was everything all wrapped up together with the pure joy of dancing – that was what audiences saw when they watched her perform.

She saw something else, too; she saw that she was good. She saw what her teachers had seen in her at the audition, and why they'd offered her the scholarship. And she saw a tiny glimpse of a future ballerina, filling *Nutcracker* audiences with Christmas joy.

Everyone clapped loudly at the end and Miss Anderbel made Tash come up and take a *révérence* – ballet-speak for curtseying and bowing – with the rest of her year. She stood next to Dani and her eyes shone with unfallen tears because she was just so *happy* that she couldn't help feeling a bit overwhelmed by it all.

"Did you like it?" whispered Dani. "It was our idea. Mine and Anisha's."

"*Thank you*," said Tash with so much awe in her voice that Dani hugged her quickly even though they were supposed to be behaving professionally and doing the *révérence* like dancers.

"I'm so proud of you," said Mum, when Tash took her seat again, and Tash knew that she didn't just mean for the dancing – she'd learned way more in her first term at Aurora House than just ballet steps.

After they'd watched the other performances, Miss Anderbel and Ms Hartley came over to talk to Mum.

"Tash's injury was such a shame," said Miss Anderbel. "She's done so well this term, we couldn't let all that wonderful dancing go to waste."

"I had no idea she could dance like that," said Mum.

"Tash is very talented," Ms Hartley said with a smile. "I'm looking forward to seeing what she can do next term, now that she's learned a thing or two. I'm beginning to think we've got a future star on our hands."

Tash listened to this praise, glowing inside. And then, once her teachers had moved on to chat to some other parents, she slipped off to stroll around the festive school with Dani and Anisha.

They weren't needed on their class stall because Donna, Laura and Toril were in charge for the next hour, but they hung around anyway, laughing at people's guesses and waiting to see everyone's reactions when the answers were announced. Lots of students and parents gathered to find out who'd won, and no one would believe that Mr Watkins was the adorable baby until he pushed through the crowd to admit that it was true. Even though Chris has guessed that the Mr Watkins photo was actually Miss Anderbel, he'd got the most right answers and was the winner of a big box of chocolates donated by Mr Kent.

After that, the fair was nearly over, and Tash, Dani and Anisha spent the rest of it wandering in and out of classrooms, playing the games on other stalls and eating ballet-themed gingerbread from Year Nine's cake stall.

"Go and look on the tree in the dining room," said Mr Kent when he saw them. "I think you'll each find something with your name on."

Tash, Dani and Anisha looked at each other for a second and then hurried to the tree as fast as Tash could go, which wasn't very fast at all. When they reached the tree in the dining room, other students were already there, searching among the branches.

"What are we looking for?" asked Tash.

"Oh, hi, guys," said Helen. "Everyone in the school has a chocolate figure with their name on it. Dani, don't take for ever to find yours. Mum and Dad want to go soon."

Tash suddenly felt a little bit sad that she and her friends wouldn't be sleeping in Coppélia that night. They'd all be in their own rooms at home, in different parts of the country.

"We should meet up in the holidays," said Anisha, while they searched.

"Yeah," said Tash. "But Dani lives so far away."

"Yes!" said Dani, pouncing on a chocolate Santa. "Oh, no, that's *Dan*." She put it back and carried on looking. "Maybe we could meet halfway? Or you guys could come and stay with me. Yes! Come and stay!"

"Yeah, that would be great! Oh! This is me," said Anisha, turning over a chocolate snowman and finding her name on a little sticker on the back.

Tash listened to the Christmas pop song that was playing on a loudspeaker and thought about all the lovely things she and Mum always did in the holidays. She couldn't wait to see Maddy and hear all about her new secondary school, and maybe she'd get to see her friends from her old dance class at home, too. She was longing to tell them all about life at ballet school. She was so excited to be going home with Mum, but three weeks without Dani and Anisha seemed like an impossibly long time. She was definitely going to make sure they managed to see each other in the holidays.

She found a gold-wrapped chocolate bear with her name on it and cradled it in her palm, thinking about everything that had happened that term. It had all nearly gone so wrong, but it had ended up being wonderful. She had the greatest friends in the world, her teachers thought she was a promising dancer, and Mum had seen what she could do after all. She loved Aurora House, and to know that she truly belonged in the place that she loved felt even better than a perfect *pirouette*.

Basic Ballet Positions

All of the wondeful ballet moves Tash, Dani and Anisha learn begin and end in one of these five basic positions...

First position
The feet point in opposite directions, with heels touching. Arms are rounded to the front.

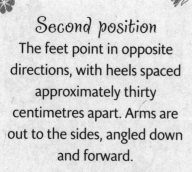

Second position
The feet point in opposite directions, with heels spaced approximately thirty centimetres apart. Arms are out to the sides, angled down and forward.

Third position
One foot is placed in front of the other so that the heel of the front foot is near the arch of the back foot. One arm is in first position, the other is in second position.

Fourth position
One foot is placed approximately thirty centimetres in front of the other. One arm is rounded and raised above the head, the other is in second position.

Fifth position
One foot is placed in front of the other, with the heel of one foot in contact with the toe of the other foot. Both arms are rounded and raised above the head.

Ballet Glossary

adage The name for the slow steps in the centre of the room, away from the barre.

arabesque A beautiful balance on one leg.

assemblé A jump where the feet come together at the end.

attitude A pose standing on one leg, the other leg raised with the knee bent.

battement glisse A faster version of *battement tendu*, with the foot lifted off the floor.

battement tendu A foot exercise where you stretch one leg out along the floor, keeping it straight all the way to the point of the foot.

chassé A soft smooth slide of the feet.

demi-pointe Dancing with the weight of the body on the toes and the ball of the foot.

développé A lifting and unfolding of one leg into the air, while balancing on the other.

en pointe Dancing on the very tips of the toes.

entrechat A jump directly upward, while crossing the feet before and behind several times in the air.

grand battement A high kick, keeping the supporting leg straight.

jeté A spring where you land on the opposite foot.

pas de bourrée Tiny little steps to the side, like a mouse.

pas de chat A cat hop from one foot to the other.

plié The first step practised in each class. You have to bend your knees slowly and make sure your feet are turned right out, with your heels firmly planted on the floor for as long as possible.

port de bras Arm movements.

révérence The curtsey at the end of class.

rond de jambe This is where you make a circle with your leg.

sissonne en arrière A jump from two feet onto one foot moving backwards.

sissonne en avant A jump from two feet onto one foot moving forwards.

soubresaut A jump off two feet, pointing your feet hard in the air.

turnout You have to stand with your legs and feet and hips all opened out and pointing to the side, not the front. This is the most important thing in ballet that everyone learns right from the start.

Usborne Quicklinks

For links to websites where you can watch
videos of ballet dancers, see excerpts of ballet
performances and find out more about ballet,
go to the Usborne Quicklinks Website at
www.usborne-quicklinks.com and enter
the keywords "ballet stars".

Tash's *Ballet Star*
dreams continue
in two more
sparkling stories...

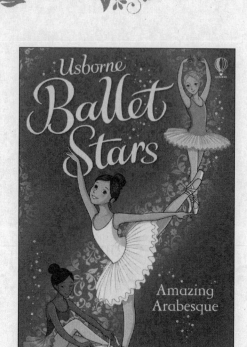

❀ Amazing Arabesque ❀

It's Tash's second term at Aurora House, and she's thrilled to be back – especially when she realizes she'll be learning to dance *en pointe*! But when Anisha starts acting strangely in class, Tash is worried. Their first ballet exam is coming up, and Anisha isn't even *trying* to master the tricky arabesque. Can Tash get her back on track before it's too late?

ISBN 9781409583547

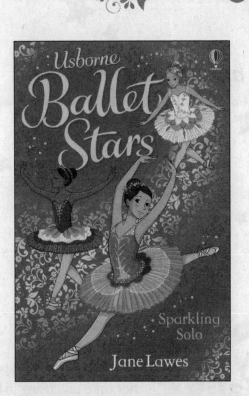

❀ Sparkling Solo ❀

It's the summer term at Aurora House and Tash is so excited about the end-of-year performance! She can't wait to dance on a real stage for the first time, and she's desperate to win the solo role of her dreams: the Lilac Fairy. But Dani is struggling with stage fright. Can Tash help her to sparkle in the spotlight?

ISBN 9781409583554

Also by Jane Lawes

Gym Stars

Summertime and Somersaults

Tara loves gym and spends all her time practising in her garden. When she joins Silverdale Gym Club she's catapulted into their star squad. But there's so much to learn. How will she ever catch up with her talented teammates?

ISBN: 9781409531791

Friendships and Backflips

Tara's training for her first ever competition and she's desperate to win a gold medal. But she's so busy learning the tricky routine that her best friends think she's deserted them. Can she find room in her life for her friends *and* gym?

ISBN: 9781409531807

Handsprings and Homework

Tara's through to a national competition, but she's training so hard that her homework is starting to pile up and she's in big trouble with her teachers. Can Tara finish all her work on time *and* win a gold medal?

ISBN: 9781409531814

For more *dazzling* reads
head to
www.usborne.com/fiction